The Vindicators

In the summer of 1879, young Ben Drake travels to the town of Mason in New Mexico. The 18-year-old aims to find out the truth about his father's death at the hands of a lynch mob, but soon the events which led to his father's death cast his own life into hazard.

Drake finds himself drawn into the Mason County War, in which a band of young men challenge the iron rule of businessman Angus McBride who seems to have the authorities at his beck and call. The confrontation culminates in the youngsters fighting against a troop of US Cavalry, in what will come to be called the Battle of Grover's Mill.

The Vindicators

Brent Larssen

A Black Horse Western

ROBERT HALE · LONDON

ISBN 978-0-7198-1648-2

Robert Hale Limited
Clerkenwell House
Clerkenwell Green
London EC1R 0HT

www.halebooks.com

Typeset by
Derek Doyle & Associates, Shaw Heath
Printed and bound in Great Britain by
CPI Antony Rowe, Chippenham and Eastbourne

CHAPTER 1

When he was an old man, Ben Drake sometimes looked back on those wild events in the fall of 1879; scarcely able to believe his own memories. The Mason County War had been a bloody incident and it had been precipitated not by conflict with the Indians or the pursuit of some particularly ruthless gang of outlaws, but by something as prosaic and unromantic as a dispute over the supply of dry goods to an obscure corner of New Mexico. Just imagine that, thought Drake to himself in later years; all those lives lost, just to settle who should be able to sell dresses, pants, pots and pans, to a bunch of farmers and cowboys! In the late summer of 1879, eighteen-year-old Ben Drake left his grandparents' house near Santa Fe and travelled south to the little town of Mason, where he had been raised. Since the age of seven, it had been drummed into Ben that his father was a no-good wastrel; a man who had kicked out his life at the end of a rope, after being lynched for rustling and the Lord knows what other low crimes and misdemeanours. His grandparents, his own mother's mother and father, had impressed all this upon him most forcibly, hinting that he too was likely to go down the self same path if he wasn't careful. These stories had never rung true for young Benjamin and were greatly at odds with what he himself recalled of his father. Now, he had come to Mason to find out the truth for his own self.

Before he set out, Ben Drake had visited the minister of their church to explain what he had in mind. This good old man had been a great support to the boy and his mother over the years. At first, the Reverend Waterhouse had been shocked, misunderstanding the purpose of his young parishioner's journey.

He said, 'If this tends towards the seeking of revenge for your father's death, then I can tell you now, it won't answer! Read the book of Romans; chapter twelve, verse nineteen. "Vengeance is mine, I will repay, saith the Lord." '

'No, sir,' said Ben, taken aback. 'I ain't about to go looking for vengeance, nor nothing of the sort. I just want to know what really happened to my pa. And if he wasn't as bad as some folks say, then maybe set things right and see the truth come out.'

'Ah,' said Reverend Waterhouse, vastly relieved. 'You want only to vindicate a dead man's name. That's quite another matter. It's a laudable enough enterprise, I'll allow.'

'I don't rightly understand you, sir,' said Ben. 'What's vindicate mean?'

'Vindicate? Why, bless you my boy, it means to clear somebody of blame, to free a body of suspicion of wrongdoing.'

'Well, I reckon that about meets the case,' said Ben, filing the strange and unfamiliar word away in his memory, for future use. 'I should think that I am hoping to vindicate my dead pa and see the truth coming out.'

Reverend Waterhouse looked at the earnest youth and his face became grave.

'You go looking for truth, son, just bear in mind that you might not like it when you've found it. But good luck to you and I'll remember you in my prayers.'

When he arrived in Mason, Ben expected to feel the stirring of familiar memories; he thought that his early childhood would all come flooding back to him. It was nothing of the sort. Sure, he recognized some of the buildings on Main Street and even remembered the general layout of the town, but none of it really meant anything to him. The town was of no greater significance to him than if it had been some place where he spent a vacation for a couple of weeks, many years ago.

The young man had never seen the inside of The Silver Dollar saloon. It was not a place where one would expect a seven-year-old boy to have visited. Well, he was no longer seven and the local saloon seemed to him as good a location as any to start his search and so within a quarter-hour of leaving the stage, Ben was sitting at the bar of The Silver Dollar, sipping a glass of porter.

The barkeep was disposed to be chatty, saying as he served Ben with his drink, 'New round here, ain't you? Leastways, I don't recollect seeing your face before.'

Young as he was, Ben Drake was not utterly devoid of sense. He knew instinctively that it would be a bad idea to broach the object of his visit to the town openly, to the first person he talked to. Instead, he decided to choose a neutral topic. He could hardly have guessed that this first casual remark of his would cut right to the heart of his mission, in a few brief words. He said, 'No, I only just arrived in these parts. Tell me, I couldn't help noticing, you only got but one store in this whole town. How come? Up my way, we've a dozen different little stores on Main Street. Our town's no bigger than this.'

The barkeep looked curiously at Ben, as though wondering how much to say. At length, he said, 'Green, ain't you? You see the name of that one store?'

'Yes, it was something like McBride.'

'The McBride Trading Company is the full name. Ain't just the store they own. Nothing so much as farts in these parts, 'less the McBrides give the go-ahead.'

'They're powerful?'

'Powerful?' said the barkeep, winking at Ben. 'Powerful? I believe you! Yeah, you might say as they're that all right.'

After the man who had served him went off to

tend to another customer, Ben mulled over what had been said. He seemed to remember his grandfather telling him about some small and out-of-the-way towns where one man and his commercial concern more or less ruled the roost. Maybe Mason was such a place. As he supped his ale, Ben listened casually to the conversations taking place at the bar on either side of him.

'Old man McBride won't wear it. . . .'

'Mark what I say, it'll end in tears. . . .'

'Said he was a rustler. . . .'

When he caught the word 'rustler', Ben Drake's ears pricked up and he turned his full attention to the two men on his left and tried his best to hear what they might be saying. But their conversation was moving on to other matters and the next thing he clearly heard was, 'Lot of damned nonsense spoke about this crop-rotation caper, if'n you ask me!'

Ben wasn't a pushy sort of youth, but thought that this was an occasion when a little brashness might be forgivable. He turned to the two men and said, 'Pardon me, did I hear something about rustling?'

'If you were eavesdropping on a private conversation, then it's very likely you did,' said an elderly man with a bristling white moustache.

This was discouraging enough, but Ben pressed on, saying, 'I have a reason for asking about rustling. I'm sorry to butt in, but could you tell me something about this rustling? Was it round here?'

The old fellow with the moustache exchanged looks with the man he had been talking with and said, 'What's it to you?'

'I knew somebody lynched for rustling near here. It was a long time ago.'

'It's not uncommon for people to shout about rustling,' said the man with the white moustache. 'There was somebody shot just a few days back. Man was supposed to have been a rustler.'

The other man, who was staring at Ben, said, 'Mind, not all those who stand accused of rustling are really guilty. And some of those who do the accusing … well, it's not the first time there's been such things that take place near this town.'

The two men turned their backs pointedly and continued talking about agricultural subjects, but Ben was tremendously excited by even this brief snatch of conversation. Unless he misread their meaning, those two men had been hinting that there had been wrongful accusations of rustling in these parts. He could hardly believe his good fortune in hearing something of this sort, so soon after fetching up in Mason.

It struck him that he would be unwise to attract further attention by pursuing the subject of rustling, so Ben thought to take a turn around the streets and then give some consideration to where he might stay that night. This last was not a big concern to the youth, because the weather was so fine that he could, at a pinch, sleep out in the open.

The town of Mason might have only the one store, but it was surely an impressive establishment. It stretched for the width of an entire block; far bigger than the average kind of store one might expect to see in a town of that size. The reason for this was pretty obvious when you looked at the variety of goods on sale there. There appeared to be nothing at all that could not be purchased in the McBride Trading Company's General Store and Emporium, as the gaudy, painted sign up by the eaves of the building proclaimed this to be.

Judging by the displays out on the front and in the windows, there was everything that one might require and all under the one roof. Brooms, zinc buckets, firewood, lamp oil, clothes, food and drink of all kinds, firearms, harnesses for horses and china tea services could all be acquired at the store; either for cash or according to 'easy terms'.

While he was standing on the boardwalk and admiring the range of goods on offer, Ben saw a troop of ponies heading along the street in his direction. He knew a little about horses and these looked to him to be tough little Indian ponies. The six ponies were roped in a line and being led along by a young man riding a taller and more elegant horse. When he saw Ben looking, this fellow shouted across the street to him.

'Hey, you looking for work? Or are you like everybody else in this town, beholden to Angus McBride?'

'I ain't beholden to nobody, nohow,' called back Ben, a little affronted. 'Who are you beholden to, if it comes to that?'

The man responded with a gale of laughter. 'You got pepper!' he said. 'Come over yonder, we can't shout our business to the whole town like this.'

As he walked up to the man on the horse, Ben said, 'Weren't aware we had any business, anywise.'

'Seriously though, you live in this town?'

'Not hardly,' replied Ben. 'Just visiting.'

'You looking for work for a bit?'

'Doin' what?'

'Helpin' to build a new store, herding cattle, all kinds of things? Where are you staying?'

'Nowhere in particular,' admitted Ben. 'I only just got here a half-hour back.'

'Well, we're looking for young men as ain't afeared o' getting their hands dirty. Problem is, nobody in this here town wants to upset the McBrides by coming to work for us. Tell you what, why don't you come out to the ranch with me and then if you don't like what you see, we ain't neither of us lost a thing.'

'This ranch, is it far from town?'

'Not a bit of it; five, maybe six miles. Can you ride bareback?'

'I have done,' said Ben. He made a snap decision. Somewhere to live and work, only a few miles from Mason, would do very well indeed. He smiled up at the other man and said, 'My name's Ben, Ben Drake.'

The rider reached down his hand and said, 'Good to know you, Ben. I'm Fenton Wilder. My friends generally call me Fen.'

As the two young men made their way north to the ranch where the ponies were being taken, Fenton

Wilder filled the other young man in on what was going on. It was not a complicated situation and it could be summed up in a few short sentences. Angus McBride and his sons operated the only store in Mason County and were also heavily involved in raising cattle and supplying the army with beef, among other enterprises in which they were involved. They operated what was, in effect, a monopoly on the sale of dry goods, tin-ware, lamp oil and various other commodities in the county and it was their aim to keep things that way.

After this had been explained to him, Ben said, 'I thought you said that you were going to be running a store? Doesn't this McBride fellow object to that?'

'Oh, he objects all right,' said Wilder laughingly, 'only there ain't a whole bunch of things he can do about it. He owns the freehold on most of the property along Main Street, so he's not about to let any rivals set up shop there, but we're starting our little place on the ranch, on our own property. There ain't a damned thing he can do to stop us.'

'Who's "us"?'

'There's a bunch of us, come down with our boss. He's bought an old ranch, with a house and some cabins for workers like us to sleep in. Now he aims to build a store and start getting the folk from Mason to ride out and buy his goods. They'll be a sight cheaper than those on offer at McBride's spot in town.'

Almost as soon as Fenton Wilder had spoken McBride's name, he and Ben trotted round a bend in the road and saw three riders heading towards them.

'Lordy,' said Wilder, 'they do say, "Speak of the Devil and he's sure to appear." Here comes McBride and his boys now.'

The riders ahead of them stopped in the road, blocking the way entirely. The man in the centre was aged about sixty or thereabouts. He had a snowy-white beard, but looked as tough as any youngster. His white beard and elderly appearance did not lend him the aspect of a favourite uncle or anything of that sort. If he resembled anything, it was one of the angrier prophets from the Bible; the kind who denounced everybody and called down fire from heaven upon their heads. He was flanked by two ill-favoured fellows who looked to be about thirty. As Wilder and Ben approached with their ponies in tow, the older man spoke, in a sharp and commanding voice.

'What are you boys about? Where are you taking those beasts?'

Fenton Wilder touched his hat and said, 'Good morning to you, Mr McBride. We're taking these ponies up to my boss's ranch. Will you hold the road against us?'

'I might,' said the old man, 'I just might damned well do that very thing. I know you, but I don't recognize that other lad, him riding bareback on the pony there. Who is he?'

Before Ben could speak for himself, Wilder said, 'His name's Ben Drake and he's a friend of mine.'

'Drake, you say? You're not from round these parts, are you, boy?'

'I don't take to being called "boy",' said Ben stoutly, 'but no, I'm not from Mason.'

The old man stared at Ben Drake for a few seconds as though he wanted to ask more questions. He contented himself in the end with saying, 'You'll do yourself no favours by getting mixed up with this crew. You looking for work? I can always use a likely-looking fellow such as yourself.'

'Thank you, sir, but I already have a job. I'm working with this man and his outfit.'

'Too bad. I woulda thought you had more sense.' The man with the white beard said to his companions, 'Come, we've more important fish to fry than these young rascals.' He and the two men with him rode forwards, and went past Wilder and Ben Drake with no more ado.

'He thinks a good deal of himself,' said Ben. 'You know him?'

'Know him? Why, that's the famous Angus McBride himself, large as life and twice as natural.'

'He sets a store by his own self from what I can make out.'

Wilder looked thoughtful and remained silent for a minute or two. Then he said, 'You know, I had the notion that McBride mighta known you. He gave you a good hard look, at any rate. You say you don't know him?'

Rather than tell his new friend a direct lie, Ben said, 'Like I said, I'm only visiting. Say, is that the ranch we're heading for, over there across the plain?'

'That it is.'

15

Memory is a strange and unreliable thing. Ben Drake would have taken oath an hour earlier that he remembered little of the town of Mason, and nothing at all about any individual person living there. But as soon as Angus McBride hove into view, Ben's heart had begun beating a little faster and he knew that this was a man that he had seen before. Not only that, this was somebody associated in the inner recesses of Ben's mind with disagreeable emotions and bad feelings. He couldn't quite call them to mind just now, although he had an idea that if he left the matter alone, the memories would before long return to him unbidden. Of one thing he had not the slightest doubt: he knew Angus McBride and the remembrance was not a pleasant one.

Chuck Taylor, who had, according to Wilder, bought the ranch and was intent on setting up a store there, came across as a good-natured and fatherly individual. That at least was the impression that Ben formed of the man, as soon as they had been introduced.

'So you want to join our little band, is that it?' said Taylor. 'Well, you're right welcome. The more men here, the better. You can use a saw and tack up a horse?'

Ben smiled. 'I can do a sight more than just those two things, sir.'

Taylor patted Ben on the shoulder affectionately. 'Good man. I'm sure you and me'll get along together well enough. Fenton here will show you where to stow your gear.'

16

It soon became clear to Ben that all the other men working for Chuck Taylor had known him for a good long time. He had been running some cattle business up near the Rockies, and for some reason, had taken it into his head to come south and combine cattle trading with setting up a store. Most of his hands had come with him to New Mexico. On the face of it, it was a smart move, at least viewed from a purely economic perspective. With only one store in the whole of Mason County, the folk living there had little choice but to pay the prices being charged by Angus McBride. Sure, they could ride a round trip of fifty miles and buy their goods elsewhere, but that would mean sacrificing a day's work. It was cheaper to pay what the McBride Trading Company's General Store and Emporium were asking.

Cornering a market in this way is every businessman's dream and Angus McBride had been in this happy position for the better part of fifteen years. Some misguided souls had, over the years, tried to break McBride's stranglehold on the commercial life of the county; but such efforts invariably came to nought. There was good reason for this. Angus McBride had lent large sums of money to the Territorial Governor, who was consequently in his pocket. The sheriff in Mason was also in the pay of the McBrides, who had put him in his job. In addition to this, the McBride Trading Company had a fair number of wild Mexican cowboys working for them; *vaqueros* who would stop at nothing, up to and including murder if the need arose. All in all, Angus

McBride and his sons had Mason County pretty well tied up and were in the habit of regarding it as their personal fiefdom. It would be a brave man, or a foolish one, who tried to rock that particular boat.

CHAPTER 2

In the course of the month that Ben Drake subsequently spent working at Taylor's ranch, he grew very fond of his boss. Chuck Taylor inspired respect in the men who worked for him; wild young men who included some of the roughest types. He never cursed at them or denounced them as idle wretches, in the way that practically every other man who employed cowboys and labourers did. Although he was perhaps twice the age of those working for him (Taylor had just turned forty-two that summer) he was always to be found in the thick of any hard work in which his men were engaged. He would strip off his shirt and chaff the boys, teasing them with the assurance that a man of his age could still lift more, dig harder and work faster than they could themselves. Nor were these empty boasts: Taylor demonstrated the truth of his claims by getting right down there with them and throwing his own weight into whatever it was that they were doing. They loved him for it.

19

Chuck Taylor had a partner in his business, a man called Patrick Sweeney. Sweeney was a rancher with a big spread, who had over the years grown weary of the way in which the McBrides ruled the roost in Mason County. By combining with Taylor, he thought that the two of them might act as a counterweight to the McBride Trading Company's domination of the region.

Before he had realized it, a month had passed and Ben was feeling altogether at home on the Taylor ranch.

Little by little, he had begun to recollect certain things from his childhood; memories which had been triggered by seeing Angus McBride. Chief among these was McBride shouting furiously at his father in their house, one night. He had vaguely retained this image of a man with a white beard yelling at his pa, but it had been so vague, indistinct and disconnected, that he had in the past wondered if it was a real event or rather something he had dreamed. However, seeing the man with the white beard in real life had brought it home to Ben most clearly that this had been no dream and that he now knew that his father had argued fiercely with the most powerful man in the county and then had later been lynched, following an accusation of cattle rustling.

He got on well with all the young men working for Chuck Taylor, but Ben had a specially soft spot for the first of the crew who he had met, which was Fenton Wilder. Wilder was a most agreeable and good-natured fellow; always ready for a lark or willing to listen to anybody's troubles. He was a universal favourite at the ranch. It therefore came as a great shock to Ben and everybody else when, a week before the new store was ready to open for business, Fenton Wilder was gunned down on the streets of Mason.

Fen Wilder was as popular among the folk in Mason as he was on the ranch where he worked. He always seemed to have a smile on his lips and one could frequently hear him coming, long before he came into sight, due to his habit of whistling a cheery tune as he strolled down the street. Angus McBride had let it be known that he viewed with extreme disfavour the fraternizing of the citizens of Mason with the boys from Chuck Taylor's ranch. Nevertheless, most people smiled at Wilder when they met him; the young man had such a pleasant and open face. Like half the men working for Taylor, he carried a pistol when in town, but he had certainly never expected to have to use it in deadly combat.

For as long as he had been running cattle in and around Mason county, Angus McBride had always shown a preference for employing Mexican *vaqueros*, rather than white Anglos. He said that his *vaqueros* worked harder than the average American cowboy, and were less apt to cause trouble. Others suggested that he paid his greasers less than the average white man would have accepted, and that they were less scrupulous about some of the more dubious tasks which McBride ordered them to undertake. Whatever the reason, groups of *vaqueros* were anything but an uncommon sight on the streets of Mason.

Not all the Mexicans seen in Mason were working for the McBride Trading Company, of course. Some of them were just passing through and others worked odd times for other outfits thereabouts; for example, Chuck Taylor's friend Sweeney.

Generally, though, if folk in town saw a bunch of *vaqueros*, they would say, 'Yon's some o' McBride's boys.' One greaser looked much the same as another to the residents of Mason.

On this particular day, Fen Wilder had come to town to visit one of his sweethearts; a little saloon girl called Belle. Truth to tell, Belle was everybody's friend and Wilder's chances of being anybody special to the girl were slim enough, but he enjoyed the challenge. He was a courtly and good-natured lover and who knew what might have developed if he'd been able to keep up his attentions for another week or two? But it was not to be.

As he strolled down Main Street in the direction of The Silver Dollar, Fenton Wilder had a song in his heart and a whistle on his lips. It was a glorious day, he was young and healthy and, more than that, he was in love. Passers-by who saw the amiable youth as he ambled along the boardwalk could not help but smile at him. He tipped his hat in greeting to men and swept his headgear entirely off for every woman. He was, in short, a pleasant sight to behold.

Evidently, not all those on the streets of Mason found Fenton Wilder an agreeable spectacle that day.

As he proceeded along the boardwalk, two men kept pace with him in the road, lagging a little behind, so that Wilder was not aware that they were dogging his footsteps. These men were nondescript-looking *vaqueros*. Fifty yards before he reached The Silver Dollar, a man who had apparently been idling and smoking ahead of him turned sharply as Wilder came nigh and moved to block his path.

'Hey, fella,' said Fen Wilder, amiably, 'any chance o' you letting me get past there?'

The olive-skinned man, Mexican by the look of him, spat and said, 'You best had walk round me. I stay here.'

Even now, Wilder didn't realize his danger. Nor was his good humour dented in the least degree. He shrugged and stepped down off the boardwalk and on to the dusty roadway. It was at this point that the two men who had been moving along behind him came and hemmed him in. With one man behind him on the boardwalk and two now crowding him from the other side, Wilder felt for the first time the faint stirring of unease.

'Can you fellows give a man a little room?' he protested lightly. 'I'm feeling powerful squashed in here.'

None of the three men spoke and neither did they move back. The one up on the boardwalk said quietly, 'Today you die.'

It was such a melodramatic thing to say, that for a moment, Wilder wasn't sure if he'd heard right. But the expression on the men's faces gradually persuaded him that he'd heard correctly and that for whatever reason, his very life was now in peril. He said meaninglessly, 'I got no quarrel with you folks. Why'nt you let me proceed down the road, peaceable like?'

'You going to draw?' asked one of the men who had been trailing him along the road. 'Will you die like a man?'

It would probably have made little difference to the eventual outcome, at least as far as his own life was concerned, but at this point, Fenton Wilder made a grave error. He went for his gun. Nobody was close enough to hear the deadly words spoken by the *vaqueros* before this happened; all they saw was the young man drawing his pistol and then the three Mexicans responding, as it seemed to this aggressive action.

If Wilder had had time to think about what was going on, he might perhaps have behaved more coolly, but the whole thing erupted so suddenly that he had no time at all to think. His pistol was not yet clear of the holster when the three other men drew and opened fire on him. When the echoes from the roar of gunfire died down, Fenton Wilder was lying dead in the road, with seven bullets in him.

The three *vaqueros* turned to face the gaping pedestrians on Main Street and one of them said loudly, 'You all see what happen. He draw on us. It was a defence.'

Then they walked briskly off, and not one of those who witnessed the episode would have been able to take oath and identify any of the three men in the future, or were even able to distinguish them in any way at all from all the other Mexican cowboys who were to be seen in and around town.

Word of Fenton Wilder's death reached Chuck Taylor's place a couple of hours later. It was brought by the Reverend Jackson, who had been on the scene a matter of minutes after the shooting. Like most everybody else in Mason, he had been familiar with the sight of the cheerful young man walking along the streets of Mason, happy as you like and with a smile for every person he met. The idea of such a youth provoking a deadly quarrel with a set of gunmen didn't set right with the minister, and he conceived it to be his duty to let the dead man's friends know what had chanced that day.

'Dead?' asked one of the boys to whom Reverend Jackson passed the sad news. 'Fen Wilder dead? It can't be, Reverend. You must be makin' some mistake.'

'It's no mistake, son. I saw the body with my own eyes. I'm sorry to be the bearer of ill tidings, but I thought you all should know. I've arranged for your friend to be taken to my church and I'll take the funeral for free, don't fret 'bout that. Maybe your boss would like to send word when he wants it. That boy had a good heart, I'm sure on it.'

Once the minister had ridden off, everybody stopped work to talk about what had happened.

'It's that bastard McBride,' said one man, 'you can be sure of it.'

'The reverend said as folk told him it was a bunch

of *vaqueros* as did this,' said another, 'and if that don't point straight to Angus McBride, I sure as hell don't know what does.'

Ben Drake had not known Wilder as long as the others and did not think it his place to venture an opinion. He had taken to Wilder and was grieved to hear of his death. At the same time, he didn't think that they should be taking hasty action; at least not without taking steps to establish the facts of the case.

The other young men did not feel inhibited by any need to conduct lengthy inquiries into what they saw as the murder of their trusted friend and comrade. For them, the case was clear. Fen Wilder had been killed by men working for Angus McBride, acting no doubt on his orders. That being so, it remained only to avenge the death. Being eager, young and hot-headed, the men went off to fetch their guns and tack up their horses. Ben hardly knew what to do. He had no horse of his own; using only those owned by Chuck Taylor. Nor did he possess a gun, never having seen the need for one and not being the sort of youth who liked swaggering around with a pistol at his hip. There was another point, though, and this was that Ben didn't share the certainty that the others had about Angus McBride being behind this business. Fen was a terrible one for the ladies; what was to stop this being the work of an aggrieved husband or father?

As he stood there indecisively, two of the men who had been quick off the mark to saddle up and arm themselves came riding up to Ben. One of them said,

'You stayin' here while we get justice for Fen? Thought you was a friend of his?'

Before Ben was able to frame an answer to this question, there came the rhythmic drumming of galloping hoofs, which signalled the arrival of Chuck Taylor. He said, 'What's to do? You boys got no work you should be carrying on with?'

Briefly, the two riders near Ben outlined the news about Wilder. Chuck Taylor listened gravely, nodding from time to time, but saying nothing. Three more men turned up on horseback; also armed to the teeth. Taylor shot them a quizzical look.

'I'm right sorry to hear about Fen. But I can't seem to make out what you fellows are about here, or where you purpose to go now?'

'We figured as Angus McBride was at the back of this. We're a-goin' to settle with him for it.'

Chuck Taylor was so easy and free with the men who worked for him in the usual way of things that his reaction now came as somewhat of a shock to them.

'You idiots!' he exclaimed angrily. 'If McBride was behind this, which is possible, I'll allow, you think he won't have made preparations for this very eventuality? You don't think he'll have sentries posted and his men all heeled? You'd be riding right into a trap.'

In the heat of their anger, this had clearly not occurred to any of the boys. Taylor continued, 'And none of you young fools can think of any other reason why somebody might have a grudge against Wilder? Really? You none of you heard where he's been hopping in and out of various beds over the last few months?'

It was plain that although all those present had been perfectly aware of Fenton Wilder's amorous exploits, not one of them had given any thought to the possibility that it was this, rather than any friction between their boss and Angus McBride, which might have been the root cause of the youngster's death.

Taylor cast his eyes around the men who, a moment earlier, had been ready and willing to ride off and deal death to Angus McBride and his men. His irritation faded and he said quietly, 'You all had a special place in your affections for that scamp. Me too. But before we start some kind of war about this, the least we can do is look into the business. Now you fellows just go and put those guns away, and get on with what needs doing. I'll join you directly.'

It was a measure of the confidence that Chuck Taylor had in his men and the regard in which they held him personally, that when he turned his mount and trotted off, Taylor knew fine well that they would all do as he had bid them.

The shooting in Mason came just a week before Chuck Taylor was ready to open his new store to the public. Calling it a store might have struck some as being just a little bit of an exaggeration. It was really two barns, which Taylor's men had been busy for the last two months converting.

They had fitted closets and shelves, turned the haylofts into storerooms and set up what approximated to a counter, dividing each barn in two. If the alterations were rough and ready, nobody was likely to notice, not once they had seen the prices being charged here. The clothes and hardware on offer in Chuck Taylor's store were being sold at about two-thirds of what they were marked up at the McBride Trading Company's Emporium in Mason. True, customers would need to take a short ride out from town to patronize the place, but it would be well worth their time and trouble to do so.

Taylor and his friend Patrick Sweeney had sunk a lot of money into the enterprise; buying quantities of cheap goods as were calculated to draw the custom of the citizens of Mason. Since the premises weren't in or even near to the town, neither Taylor nor Sweeney could see any way in which Angus McBride or his sons could have any effect upon the business.

Fenton Wilder's funeral was held the day before Taylor and Sweeney's General Store was scheduled to open up at Chuck Taylor's spread. The sheriff in Mason, who was in any case the McBrides' creature, was on sure ground when he ruled that this was an open and shut case of self-defence. He had obtained signed statements from three men who had been on the street that day, and swore that Fen Wilder drew down on a group of unknown Mexicans, who then proved to be quicker on the draw than the young man. It was tragic, but certainly not a matter for the sheriff's office to investigate.

Both Chuck Taylor and Patrick Sweeney made discreet inquiries of their own, but nobody seemed to know any more than that Wilder had had a run-in with some men and died as a consequence. The men concerned had either not been seen in town since or, if they had, had not been recognized. There was little point in launching a range war on such flimsy grounds, it being altogether possible that the young man's death was nothing to do with McBride.

It had been a while since Ben Drake had attended a funeral. Come to think of it, he realized with a shock, this was the first time he had even set foot in church since fetching up in Mason. His grandparents were red-hot for church-going, which had naturally put him off it since he had grown up a little.

The service was pleasant enough and the church full. The familiar words of the prayers came easily enough to Ben's lips, but he found that he didn't believe a word of them. It wasn't in reason to suppose that Fen was really sitting up in heaven now, in the company of the saints and apostles. How could anybody believe such foolishness?

The opening of the store was a grand affair, with crowds of folk arriving not just from Mason, but also from the farms for some miles around. For too long, Angus McBride had ruled the roost and charged what he pleased in his grand emporium. People were right pleased to find that they now had a choice in where they spent their cash.

It wasn't in reason that any man, let alone one as ruthless and unprincipled as Angus McBride, should stand by and watch the monopoly that he had carefully built up over so many years, shattered overnight. McBride had not got where he was by taking hasty and precipitate action. He had planned his counter move against Chuck Taylor from the moment he heard what that man had in mind. He first waited to see what the popular reaction would be to the rival store, and when he found that it was bidding fair to take much of his custom, McBride struck.

The McBride Trading Company's influence reached up into Santa Fe, and the Territorial Governor there was heavily in Angus McBride's debt. Since the Governor appointed the judges, this gave McBride an edge in legal matters conducted up in the territorial capital. McBride had already initiated a case against Patrick Sweeney, some weeks before the opening of the store. He claimed that Sweeney owed him over $10,000 and that because he refused to settle his debts, the courts should order an attachment against any horses and other livestock kept up at Sweeney's ranch.

If things had been all in order and above board, of course, Sweeney would have been served with notice of all this and given the opportunity to lodge a defence with the court, or even to make a counter-claim. As it was, McBride had managed to fix things so that the subpoenas and summonses were not actually served, although affidavits were filed at the court in Santa Fe, proving that this had in fact been done.

It took a while after the opening of Taylor and Sweeney's store before Angus McBride decided that this posed a real and credible threat to his own business interests. Then there was a delay, as wires went backwards and forwards between Mason and Santa Fe. The upshot was, though, that Angus McBride got his writ, a distress warrant which allowed him to seize all the assets and chattels of Patrick Sweeney, up to the value of $10,000. The next step was enforcing the thing, which would, thought Angus McBride to himself, put an end to this damned nonsense once for all. Because the writ was a legal document, and seeing that Sheriff Joe Palmer only held his post by virtue of the support which the McBride Trading Company had given him, it was plain to Angus McBride what should happen after that.

Joe Palmer wasn't at all keen on what was suggested to him in the privacy of his office.

'Hell, Mr McBride,' he said, when the scheme had been set out before him, 'I can't do that! I don't care for Sweeney any more than you, but when all's said and done, I don't believe that he's been given the chance to settle with you on these "debts". Any road, when did you lend Patrick Sweeney $10,000? I never heard about this before.'

'You're hearing about it right this minute, Joe. All I'll need is a posse to attach his goods and take any livestock on his land. It's all above board and legal, there's the judge's seal on the writ.'

'It won't answer,' said Palmer stubbornly. 'To levy on a distress warrant like that, I'd need a dozen deputies. Nobody in this town's likely to sign up for such a thing. Pat Sweeney's pretty popular round here.'

Angus McBride appeared to consider this point for a spell. Then he said, 'Ah, there, I fancy, I can help you.'

CHAPTER 3

In the end, Joe Palmer did as he was told, because he knew that McBride had the ear of the Territorial Attorney-General as well as that of the Governor in Santa Fe. Not to mention where he owed his own appointment as sheriff to Angus McBride. He wasn't easy in his mind about the affair, but there seemed little enough to be done about it. He arranged to meet McBride outside town the next day, so that they could ride over to Patrick Sweeney's ranch and levy distress on his goods.

The sheriff had examined the writ issued in Santa Fe and it was, he had to concede, a properly issued and legally binding document; no matter how it had been obtained. It laid upon him, Joe Palmer, a duty to assist in removing $10,000 worth of goods and chattels from Sweeney's place. McBride had promised to provide the men necessary to enforce the thing, but to comply with the legal niceties, Sheriff Palmer would need to deputize all the men involved. He'd no wish to do this in his office, which might have alerted one of Sweeney or Taylor's men to what was in the wind. If this was to be accomplished, then the way to do it was to swoop down on the Sweeney spread and take what was needful swiftly and neatly, by main force.

It was when he first set eyes upon the men that he was expected to swear in as deputies that it dawned on Joe Palmer precisely what a crooked piece of work he had become mixed up in. There were fourteen of them waiting with Angus McBride and his two sons, and every mother's son of them were *vaqueros* of the wildest appearance. All the men with the McBrides were heavily armed, and Palmer thought that never in all his born days had he set eyes on such a villainous-looking rabble as this. They looked like a regular set of bandits.

'Mr McBride, may I have a confidential word?' asked Palmer. When the two of them had moved out of earshot of the others, the sheriff said, 'You really want that I should deputize all these fellows?'

'Yes, what else?'

'I don't know, sir. I don't know these men. They ain't householders or nothing of the sort.'

Angus McBride rode his horse up close enough to Palmer's that their knees were brushing. Then he leaned over so that their faces were only twelve inches or so apart and said, 'I set you in that post and I can tip you off it again soon enough. That what you want?'

'No, of course not. It's just that. . . .'

McBride cut in with great irritation and said, 'You

with me or agin me, Palmer? Straight choice, it's up to you.'

When the case was set out as bluntly as that of course, it was really no choice at all. Who, in his right mind, would decide to stand against Angus McBride and all the power that was behind him and his company?

'I'm with you, sir,' said Sheriff Palmer.

The fourteen men working for the McBride Trading Company were deputized en masse; which was in itself a mite irregular. Not that anybody other than they, the McBrides and Joe Palmer himself, were ever likely to know aught of the precise circumstances. The only one of the men who Palmer knew by sight was the foreman, whose name, improbably enough, was given as Francis Xavier. Once the swearing in had been undertaken, the whole body of them set off to Patrick Sweeney's ranch.

So far, Palmer was thinking, he had been party to nothing which couldn't be explained away, should the need arise. It was when they came across Chuck Taylor and one of his boys escorting a string of ponies that Sheriff Palmer's worst fears were realized.

Patrick Sweeney's involvement in the store was chiefly that of sleeping partner. His time was fully occupied with ranching and although he was by way of being an old friend of Taylor's, he didn't really want to be actively concerned with the project. Sweeney had fish of his own to fry right at that moment: he was investigating rumours that in order to fulfil his contract to supply the army with beef,

Angus McBride had been rustling cattle himself. Since he was always the first to accuse others of this and had been instrumental in a number of lynchings for that very offence, Sweeney was intrigued by the idea that it was really McBride himself who was up to those tricks.

When the posse, which was nominally under the command of Sheriff Palmer, came upon Chuck Taylor, he was leading nine ponies away from Sweeney's place. These were loaded up with provisions for the store. Riding alongside Chuck Taylor was a boy called Ralph Moore. Ralph was devoted to Taylor and had been pleased earlier that day to be asked to accompany the boss to Sweeney's place. As the two of them rode along with the heavily laden ponies, they were both feeling light-hearted and gay.

It was young Ralph who saw the line of horsemen ahead of them. He said, 'Look, sir. Ain't that the sheriff with those men?' He was about to add that he could see Angus McBride and his foreman as well, but Taylor cut in right sharp and spoke with an urgency.

'Ralph, you ride off now. Fast as you like and make for home.'

The boy stared at him uncomprehendingly, and Chuck Taylor reached out and slapped the rump of his horse, saying, 'Go on now, ride!'

Hardly knowing what was happening, but in the habit of following Taylor's orders, the youngster spurred on his mount and headed off, away from the oncoming riders.

As soon as Angus McBride recognized Taylor as the man in charge of the ponies, he knew that he had just had the most tremendous stroke of luck and that he was now in a position to deal with another of his difficulties without a lot of fuss and bother. Having Patrick Sweeney poking about into the ways in which the McBride Trading Company acquired its steers had precipitated McBride's action through the Santa Fe court, but now there was a golden opportunity to kill two jackrabbits with one shot. McBride turned to Joe Palmer and said, 'Those ponies are coming from Sweeney's spread, I'll be bound. This is an attempt to hide his goods and defeat the ends of justice. You see for yourself what's going on. He'll be hiding all his livestock on Chuck Taylor's ranch, so you can't seize it. Those two are as thick as thieves.'

'Hey, I don't know about that,' said the sheriff uneasily. 'We got no legal right to take anything 'cept what's actually on Sweeney's land. I can't just guess where Taylor got his ponies and seize 'em from him.'

Palmer smiled nervously at the grim-faced old man at his side, hoping that he'd made his position plain about this. Why, he thought, it'd be tantamount to highway robbery if they were to ride down on Taylor now and take those beasts from him! It was a measure of Sheriff Palmer's fairly decent but essentially weak nature that his thoughts should turn to nothing worse than robbery at that moment.

As the posse drew closer to the string of ponies, one of the men riding alongside the ponies suddenly galloped off. Two of McBride's *vaqueros* started forwards, thinking perhaps to head him off, but at a shouted command from Angus McBride, they reined in and rejoined the others. Chuck Taylor had stopped now and was evidently waiting for the men to come close enough to exchange words with them. He seemed to be quite at his ease; he didn't look at all to Joe Palmer like a man who was up to no good. Besides which, he knew Taylor to be an honest, if tough, fellow. Palmer, like everybody else in Mason, was aware of the friction between Chuck Taylor and Angus McBride over the new store, but that was merely a matter of business.

'Morning, McBride,' called Taylor, as they came within hailing distance. 'Sheriff, good to see you. What brings you all out here? Nothing amiss, I hope?'

'Those ponies are Patrick Sweeney's property,' announced Angus McBride loudly. 'Sheriff Palmer here has a distress warrant, meaning that he can take anything belonging to Sweeney.'

Chuck Taylor had had a slight premonition of trouble, which was why he'd sent young Ralph Moore off, but this was quite unexpected.

'The hell are you talking about? These ponies are mine. They're nothing to do with Sweeney. Sheriff, are you a party to this?'

'I got a writ as was issued in Santa Fe. Gives me a duty to help levy distress on Patrick Sweeney's goods. That includes livestock,' said Palmer miserably. He knew now that McBride had played him for a fool and that he was presently up to his neck in something which was likely to end very badly. He continued, 'Listen, Mr Taylor, why don't you just let me and the men here check out those ponies and see what's what? Happen it's all a misunderstanding.'

'Misunderstanding is about right,' said Chuck Taylor slowly. 'My understanding 'til now was that your job is upholding the law. Looks like I was wrong, since you're now acting like some kind of road agent.'

At this accusation, Joe Palmer blushed deep crimson like a schoolgirl. Taylor had hit him where it hurt, and the words he spoke mirrored just exactly what Palmer himself was thinking. He struggled to frame a reply, but before he could do so, McBride's foreman rode forwards and peered closely at the lead pony.

He looked up and announced firmly, 'I know this creature. I see it before at Sweeney's ranch.'

'What are you talking about?' asked Taylor, his bewilderment obvious. 'When were you ever at Patrick Sweeney's spread? He would have turfed you out soon as he set eyes on you.'

The man who called himself Francis Xavier announced slowly and clearly, as though he had been coached in the form of words to use, which was in fact the case, 'I was there when Mr McBride lent $10,000 to Sweeney.'

'What nonsense is this? I never heard the like. Why would Pat borrow $10,000 from your boss?' Taylor turned to Palmer and said, 'Sheriff, don't tell me you're going to go along with this foolishness?'

'Says here on the writ that Mr McBride lent Patrick Sweeney $10,000. You'd best take it up with the court in Santa Fe. I ain't authorized to investigate the matter now.'

While this conversation was taking place, the *vaqueros* were, at a discreet signal from Angus McBride, fanning out and surrounding Taylor and the ponies. Sheriff Palmer had a horrible feeling that things were slipping out of his control. As for Taylor, he decided that this had gone quite far enough, and he wasn't going to be pushed around and deprived of his own belongings, especially when the whole thing was based on such a lie as that. The idea of Sweeney borrowing thousands of dollars from McBride was so obviously a bare-faced falsehood. He reached down to pull the rifle from where it nestled in the scabbard by his knee.

Joe Palmer saw this action and moaned, 'No, no, for Christ's sake, don't do that!' It was too late.

Before Taylor had even pulled his rifle clear of the scabbard, three or four of the Mexicans had already reacted. The truth was, Taylor didn't think that he was taking part in some showdown or gunfight; he only intended to cradle the weapon in his arms to indicate that he was not about to be pushed round by these people. Angus McBride said a few words in Spanish to his foreman and then there was a single shot. Sheriff Palmer watched in slowly fading disbelief as a neat hole appeared in the front of Chuck Taylor's plaid shirt. Then there was a fusillade of shots, too many to count individually; the roar of gunfire melding together like a rumbling clap of thunder. Taylor fell backwards off his horse, which then bolted in terror, dragging its rider along by a foot tangled in the stirrup.

As abruptly as it had begun, the shooting ended and in the eerie silence which followed, the sheriff heard McBride remark with satisfaction, 'Well, I guess that finishes that.'

Up on a ridge of high ground, two miles away, Ralph Moore heard the shooting and paused to look back. At that distance, he couldn't see much, but he certainly knew that something terrible had happened to the boss. He spurred on his horse and galloped off towards Taylor's ranch. He was eager to tell the other hands what had occurred, but there was also an element of self-interest in the case: he guessed that some of those greasers might be dispatched to silence the only witness to what he strongly suspected would turn out to be a murder.

Sheriff Palmer stared in horror at the scene. One of the *vaqueros* had fetched Taylor and his horse back to where the posse was waiting. The foreman dismounted and disentangled the dead man's foot from the stirrup. Most of the bullets had taken Chuck Taylor in the chest, but two had hit him in the face. One of these had struck him a little below his left eye, which had as a result been blown clear of its socket. It hung down on the cheek, looking to the sheriff's eyes like an over-ripe grape.

'Oh, God,' he groaned. 'What will we do? Why did they kill him?'

'You saw him going for his gun,' said Angus McBride. 'They were acting in self-defence. It was plain as a pikestaff. Don't be such a girl.'

'I'll have to write up a report on this. A man's dead.'

'Yes,' said McBride, 'a man who was dealing in stolen property, trying to hide another man's assets from the court. You're a law officer, you ought to be glad we got him. Anyway, they're your deputies, so you alone are answerable. If you didn't trust them, you shouldn't have deputized them in the first place.'

This aspect of the thing had not yet occurred to Palmer, but now he considered it, there was something in what McBride said. It was in his own best interests to help cover up what had happened here. After all, he had deputized those damned Mexicans. He said, 'This needs thinking on. I have to get back to Mason now.'

'You best think on your own future while you're about it,' said McBride. 'No reason why you and me should fall out here. Mind, though, I tell you for now, if we do, then things are likely to get damned hot. You take my meaning?'

Ralph Moore's news created a sensation, with most every one of the young men who worked for Chuck Taylor getting ready to ride off at once and rescue him from his enemies.

It was Ben Drake who managed to stop this, by saying, 'If what Ralph here tells us is true, then I'd say the boss is already dead.'

'Then what?' said another boy. 'You think we should let those bastards get away with it?'

'I don't say so,' said Ben patiently, 'I'm thinking as we ought to take advice from somebody who knows about these things.'

'What, the law? You heard what Ralphie said. Sheriff Palmer was there as well.'

'No, I was thinking of Mr Sweeney. Him and the boss are right good friends. He'll know what's right.'

From the look on their faces, it was plain that none of the others had thought of taking this step. They were so fired up with the lust for vengeance that seeking a little bit of impartial advice was the last thing on their minds.

'It can't do any harm,' said Ben. 'Mr Sweeney'll help us, like as not.'

In the end, it was agreed that every one of them would ride off at once to Sweeney's ranch.

Having killed the man who was the driving force behind the store which promised to break his monopoly on the county's trade, Angus McBride was now in no hurry to go up against Sweeney and his men. He figured that he had accomplished enough for one day. With Taylor dead, the store would most likely fold up in any case and that had been his main concern. He was well aware that Patrick Sweeney had men sniffing round, trying to find evidence of rustling or other sharp practice.

That could wait, though. One killing was as much as that soft fool Palmer could be expected to countenance in one day. More than that today and there was always a slender chance that the man would revolt and take the Lord knows what action on his own initiative.

'All right, you men, now listen up,' said McBride. 'We've finished now for this day, at least as far as this affair goes. There's a heap of work to do back at my place. Sling Taylor over his horse and we'll take his body to town. Leastways, some of you men can do so.'

'What'll we do with him when we get to Mason?' one man was incautious enough to inquire.

'You can take him to The Silver Dollar and stand him a drink,' snarled McBride angrily. 'Why, you fool, I don't much care what you do with the cow's son. Dump him in the middle of Main Street for all I care. I just want every man in Mason to see what happens to those who set up in opposition to me.'

Patrick Sweeney was standing outside his house when he saw in the distance a troop of what looked to be at least twenty riders galloping hell for leather towards his property. His first thought was, not unnaturally, that these were men working for Angus McBride who had been sent to murder him. He knew that McBride would have some inkling that his dealings with cattle were now under covert investigation and he was the kind of man to take that very ill. Without further ado, Sweeney darted into the house and took the loaded Winchester that he always had lying ready at hand. Then he went back out on to the porch to see what would develop. His hands were all at work and if this truly was a gang of men intent on harming him, then he was altogether lost. The most he could hope for was to take one or two of them with him.

As the troop of riders approached, Sweeney saw to his relief that he recognized one or two of them. They were Chuck Taylor's boys. Relief washed through him; it is always pleasing to discover that you are not, after all, about to die a bloody and violent death. He walked forward to meet the men.

'Well,' he said, 'what's the case? Why aren't you boys about your work? Wait 'til Taylor finds you making holiday, he'll let you know all about it!'

'It's about Mr Taylor that we've come, sir,' said Tim Johnson, a man of perhaps twenty-three; one of the oldest of Taylor's boys. 'We think he's been killed.'

'The hell he has! What makes you think so?'

Johnson ushered forwards young Ralph Moore, who explained what had happened, and what he had seen and heard. After he had spoken, Sweeney said nothing for a space and then announced, 'You boys stay here. I'll ride into town and see what's being said.'

'You want that some of us should ride with you?' asked Tim Johnson.

'No,' said Sweeney at once, 'this is a time for cool heads. I don't want any of you youngsters doing anything. Leastways, not 'til we know if there's aught needs doing.' He went off to the nearby barn and fetched out a saddle and bridle. After he'd brought his horse in from the field and tacked her up, Sweeney said once again, 'I don't want one of you fellows to leave this ranch. You all pledge your honour on it?'

There were nods and grunts of agreement, upon which Patrick Sweeny mounted and set the mare off at a canter towards Mason.

Even the rough and ready Mexicans working for Angus McBride baulked at simply dumping a corpse unceremoniously in the middle of town. Devout, if unobservant, Catholics to a man, they had a superstitious dread of the dead, so they carried Chuck Taylor's lifeless body to the church and laid it carefully outside the gate to the burying ground. This action was observed by a number of folk in town, who didn't feel inclined to challenge the men and ask where they had acquired their grisly load. When the *vaqueros* had ridden off, people gradually drifted over to see whose body this was. It was recognized almost immediately, and there was intense and prolonged speculation about what this could all mean.

By the time that Patrick Sweeney hit town, Taylor's body had been carried into the church itself and placed on a trestle table. Even the minister himself appeared at a loss to know how to deal with such an unexpected arrival. Word had been sent to Sheriff Palmer, but he was not in his office and nobody knew where he was or when he'd be back. Until he returned, nobody could think of any more fitting place for the bullet-riddled corpse than to leave it lying on that table in the church.

As soon as he rode into Mason, Sweeney could tell that something out of the ordinary had happened. People were standing in little huddled clusters, talking in low voices. When they caught sight of him, they fell silent. He knew then that what Taylor's boys had told him was almost certainly true. The Silver Dollar acted as an information exchange, and it was to there that Sweeney directed his steps and soon learned the grim news from the barkeep. His heart filled with dread anticipation, Sweeney left the saloon, his mare tethered to the hitching post, and made his way to the church. From far off, he could see that although it was a week day, the church looked to be having a constant stream of visitors.

CHAPTER 4

The exhibition of a bloody corpse in the little church was such a novelty as to ensure that many in the town found their way to church that Tuesday afternoon. When Patrick Sweeney was glimpsed, striding purposefully towards the place of worship, there was a discreet hurry to leave. Nobody wished to appear ghoulish, not with the dead man's friend about to arrive. The church was accordingly quite empty when Sweeney entered it.

The dead man just fitted neatly on to the trestle table, which was more commonly used for outdoor barbecues than serving in this fashion as an impromptu bier. Somebody, Sweeney guessed the minister, had lit two candles and left them burning near Taylor's head. He was not an emotional man, but Patrick Sweeney was almost overcome with grief when he saw the indisputable evidence of his friend's death. Not having yet received the ministrations of a mortician, the corpse had a hideous aspect, with one eye hanging out of its socket.

Sweeney had encountered death in many forms during the war, but nothing had ever affected him in this way. He rubbed his eyes, shook his head and then left the church in search of Sheriff Palmer, to see what steps would be taken to hunt down the men who had done this. From the number of bullet wounds, it was pretty plain to Sweeney that his friend had been attacked by a gang of men, rather than jumped by a lone assassin.

As chance would have it, Sweeney reached the sheriff's office at pretty much the same moment that Joe Palmer returned from his wanderings. The sheriff had not gone straight back to Mason after the killing, but had instead gone off alone to reason matters out.

Deep inside, the sheriff knew that he had allowed himself to become mixed up in something downright criminal. He did not believe for a single moment that Patrick Sweeney had borrowed $10,000 from McBride, and nor did he think that Chuck Taylor had been threatening to kill anybody when he was gunned down by those damned greasers. Truth was, he had witnessed a cold-blooded murder and done nothing either to prevent it or bring the perpetrators to justice after the event.

These were sobering reflections and the sheriff of Mason County knew that somewhere down the line, he must have taken a wrong turning to find himself in a position where he felt himself obliged to turn a blind eye to such goings-on. He knew that he had accepted Angus McBride's assistance in securing his

50

present post, and that he had repaid the favour by not being strictly impartial when dealing with the McBrides, but he had never looked to find himself embroiled in covering up a murder.

It was in this low frame of mind that Joe Palmer, as he dismounted outside his office, saw Patrick Sweeney walking purposefully towards him. This promised to be a trying interview, to say the very least of it.

'Sheriff Palmer,' said Sweeney firmly but politely, 'there's a man lying dead in the church down the street. He was a friend of mine, but that's nothing to the purpose. I hear he was dumped here by a bunch of *vaqueros*.'

'I know all about it, Mr Sweeney,' replied Palmer, with an air of confidence and authority that he was very far from feeling within. 'I'm dealing with this. You don't need to involve yourself.'

'You mean you're on the track of those responsible?'

'I mean it's law business. You're a private individual and it's for me to decide what happens next.'

Something about Joe Palmer's attitude rang false. Sweeney said, 'Are you investigating this death or not?'

The façade slipped a little and the sheriff of Mason County looked a little shifty and evasive. Then he blustered, saying, 'I don't answer to you, Mr Sweeney. The boot's on the other foot. Now if you'll let me get into my office, I've work to do, even if you haven't.'

'What aren't you telling me? Do you know who killed Taylor?'

'I do.'

'When are you going after them?'

'I'm not, as you put it, "going after them". Far as I can gauge, there's no crime been committed.'

Patrick Sweeney could hardly believe his ears. 'No crime? What the hell are you talking about?'

'Don't come here cursing and blaspheming,' said Sheriff Palmer prissily, 'there ain't no call for it. There's no crime, because that friend of yours was killed by a duly appointed deputy.'

'What deputy?' asked Sweeney incredulously. 'You don't have a deputy.'

'I authorized some men this very day to help me in a specific case I was handling. Taylor, God rest him, drew down on them and he was shot. There's no more to be said. I'm sorry and all, but there it is. He shouldn't have gone for his gun.'

'You going to tell me more about this?'

'It concerns you, Mr Sweeney. I don't think that it would be proper for me to do so. You best consult your attorney, if you have one. I got nothing more to say on it.'

It wasn't really necessary for Palmer to say any more, because Patrick Sweeney had already put together the pieces of the puzzle, as he was talking to the sheriff. It was common knowledge that Joe Palmer owed his very job to Angus McBride. Add to that, he knew it had been *vaqueros* who had left Taylor's body in town, and that the sheriff had admitted that he had deputized some men that very day, therefore the whole thing added up to a conspiracy against him and Chuck Taylor.

It was no surprise to Sweeney that the McBrides had taken some action against him and his friend and business partner; he had been expecting some trouble from that quarter. But that it had taken the form of a murder was unexpected. He would have thought that Angus McBride was more one for mis-using legal processes, rather than just ordering his men to kill an enemy like this. Then Sweeney recol-lected what Joe Palmer had said about deputizing men in a matter which affected Sweeney himself. He didn't know the details, but it struck Patrick Sweeney that the sooner he was off the streets of Mason and back on his own territory, the safer he'd feel.

When Taylor's boys saw Patrick Sweeney riding back from town, they hoped in their hearts that he would tell them that the whole thing had been a ludi-crous mistake, and that their boss was alive and well; mad as hell at them for abandoning their work on account of some silly rumour. When he was close enough for them to mark the expression on his face, this hope faded and died. They could see at once that their worst fears had been realized.

'Well, sir,' called one of the younger men, who was barely eighteen years of age, 'did you find out any-thing?'

The ranch owner reined in his horse and dis-mounted before replying. Then he said, 'Some of you boys go and round up my men. Tell 'em to drop what they're about and come to the house at once. The rest of you, come with me.'

When Ralph Moore and another youngster had gone to look for Sweeney's men, he said to the others, 'I'll tell you now, there's no doubt that your boss is dead.'

'How d'you know?'

' 'Cause I saw his corpse, that's how.'

'Had he been shot, like Ralphie said?'

'He'd been shot all right. A dozen times. And it was McBride's men who did it as well. No doubt about that either.' In as few words as possible, Sweeney set out for them what he'd seen in town and also the gist of his conversation with Sheriff Palmer. There was a stunned silence.

'You mean sheriff's in on it?' asked somebody.

'Not willingly, maybe. I'm guessing as McBride's hooked him in on some legal thing. I don't rightly know what. But Palmer's not a bad fellow. I'd say he's in over his head here.'

'What do we do now?' asked Ben Drake. 'Do we go back to the store or what?'

It was now that Patrick Sweeney unfolded to the young men who were gathered around him in a circle the idea which had been fermenting in his mind on the way back from town. Had he but known it, the plans that Sweeney set out to those hot-headed youths were to trigger what later was known as the Great Mason County War, although that was the last thing in Sweeney's mind. He only sought justice for his murdered friend and also hoped to make provision for these young fellows who had suddenly been deprived of both a good friend and their jobs; all at one fell swoop. They do say that the road to hell is paved with good intentions, and Patrick Sweeney's intentions that afternoon could hardly have been better.

'I know you boys are grieved about this,' said Sweeney. 'Some o' you saw Taylor like a father, I know that. But we need to think now on how we can bring those as killed him to justice.'

'You mean like vigilante justice?' asked Ben. ''Cause from all I apprehend, you're saying the sheriff had a hand in Mr Taylor's death. I reckon that means that we can't go to law over it.'

'You're a smart one,' said Sweeney admiringly, 'but no, all the same I ain't talking of vigilantes nor nothing of the sort. Palmer deputized some of those *vaqueros* as work for McBride, if I understand the situation correctly. But it was a crooked business for all of that. Two can play at that game. I'm wondering how you boys would feel about being deputized yourselves? You'd get a dollar a day and I can't see any reason why you couldn't carry on living over at Chuck Taylor's place. Hell, you could even keep running the store, maybe.'

The youngsters looked at each other, unsure what to make of this notion. It was Ben Drake who asked, 'How would that work, Mr Sweeney? Meaning, how could we become deputies?'

'Sheriff Palmer's not the only law in Mason County. Sure, he's county sheriff, but there're justices as well, justices of the peace. Then again, there's a town a few miles from here that has a constable.

He's regular law. These are men I know and trust. I'll warrant I can get them to swear you men in and then you could legally arrest those men who killed your boss.'

This was all doubly pleasing for the boys who had been working for Chuck Taylor. On the one hand, they were all genuinely grief-stricken at the death of a man that they all loved and respected. Then again, there was an element of selfishness bound up in it all, because with Taylor dead, most of them didn't know where their money would be coming from. Some of them had been with Chuck Taylor for years; even before he relocated to New Mexico. Sorry though they'd been to learn of his death, they were also anxious for their immediate future.

'You think as you could do that for us, sir?' asked Tim Johnson. 'Have us sworn in and paid as deputies, I mean.'

'I'm damned sure I can. There's one or two favours to call in, but yes, I think I can swing it. Angus McBride ain't the only one hereabouts that can exert undue influence in such matters.'

That night, Sweeney invited the fellows from Chuck Taylor's ranch to stay and eat with his own men, hunkering down for the night afterwards as best they could in the bunkhouses and barns. The next day, he roused them early and chose three men to accompany him on a little trip. Ben Drake was one of these; the other two were Tim Johnson and a boy they all called Horse, because of his prodigious strength.

'You others,' said Sweeney before they left, 'try and make yourselves useful around the place. My boys'll show you what needs doing. You know they say that the Devil makes mischief for idle hands.' The young men laughed at this, telling each other later that that Mr Sweeney was a real card.

It was a good morning to be out and about on horseback. The sky was as blue as robins' eggs and there wasn't a cloud to be seen. They rode north and after a time, Ben asked how far they would be going.

'Only twenty miles or so,' said Sweeney. 'You know a little hamlet called Fiddler's Creek?'

'Heard of it,' said Johnson, 'never been there, though.' The other two shook their heads.

'Only a dozen families live there now. Used to be a fair-sized town for a while, after they struck silver. Then the lodes ran dry and everybody moved on elsewhere. It's near as damn a ghost town now. But anyways, you fellows don't want a history lesson. Fact is, they have a town constable still, old friend of mine. He's more or less retired now, getting on a mite in years. But he still has as much authority as a regular sheriff or marshal. More than that, there's a justice of the peace living nigh to Fiddler's Creek. That's another happy circumstance.'

Back in Mason, Joe Palmer was not having an easy time of it. Angus McBride and his two sons had come calling on him at home, before the sun had hardly risen.

'All right, all right,' he said, as the hammering on his door intensified, 'I'm coming.'

57

He opened the door and was then compelled to step back smartly as Angus McBride pushed past him. His two boys, who were the meanest pair of bastards that Palmer knew or ever had heard of, followed their pa into his home without so much as a by-your-leave.

'Make yourselves at home,' muttered Palmer, as his visitors led the way to his kitchen.

'I hear where you were shooting the breeze with Pat Sweeney yesterday, after we parted company,' said Angus McBride. 'Care to tell us what you said to him?'

'Nothin' much. He wanted to report Taylor's death to me. Told him I already knew all about it.'

'Ah. What did he say to that?'

'Didn't say nothing much. Just lit out.'

'You didn't maybe tip him the wink that we might be coming to take his stock?'

Sheriff Palmer shook his head. 'No, 'course not. I'm as deep in this as you. I wish to God it weren't so, but it is. You and me swim or sink together.'

To his surprise, McBride gave him a wide, friendly grin and said, 'Maybe I was wrong about you. I reckon you understand how we're situated as well as I do.' He turned to his sons and said, 'Come on. We got work to do.' As he headed down the hallway, McBride turned back and said to Sheriff Palmer, 'Sorry for troubling you. Let me know if Sweeney comes sniffing round again. Secrets make me nervous.'

When the three men had gone, Palmer found to

his chagrin that he was all covered in sweat. One of the McBrides alone was enough to make him uneasy; the three of them together like that was almost more than flesh and blood could endure. He truly was beginning to wonder since yesterday's little adventure if the game was worth the candle any more. Maybe he'd do better just digging up and starting afresh somewhere on his own account. But then, he was thirty-eight years of age. The prospect of starting anywhere from scratch was not an enticing one.

Constable Ballard had kept order in Fiddler's Creek when it was a boom town during the great silver rush of the forties. Now, there were only a handful of folk left in the place and most of them were, like Ballard, getting on in years. Visitors to the town were rare enough these days and to see three ride in together was almost unheard of. One of them turned out to be an old friend from way back: Pat Sweeney.

'Pat, you old bastard,' cried Constable Ballard, rising from the rocking chair on his porch, 'what brings you to these here parts?'

'Hallo, Sam. How's it going?'

'Quiet. Mighty quiet. Who're your friends?'

'These youngsters? Why, they're your new deputies!'

'Deputies? I don't need no deputies. Ain't work enough for one constable, never mind deputies! What is this, Pat?'

Briefly, Patrick Sweeney explained what was going on and old Sam Ballard pulled a face. 'McBride up to his old tricks again, hey? This sounds worse than his usual games, though. So you want these boys to be authorized to bring in those that killed your friend, is that the way of it?'

'Pretty much, yes. There's another eighteen of these young rogues. You give me a commission to do so and I can then deputize them as well.'

'You want me to swear out warrants for McBride and his boys?'

'No, I thought I'd get that justice to do it, you know who I mean. Kershaw.'

Constable Ballard scratched his head. 'So all you want me to do is swear in you and these three boys as deputies and my role in the matter's done, is that the strength of it?'

' 'Part from their fees. Dollar a day, isn't it? You give me the paperwork, I can recover the money from the Mason County Commissioners.'

'Yeah, yeah. Come inside now and I'll get the job done. Then maybe you'll leave me in peace for another year. You ain't come near nor by me for a twelvemonth, Pat Sweeney. Only time I ever see you is when you're after something.' The old man stood up and beckoned them. 'Come into my lair, now.'

Ben wondered if they were about to be offered coffee or even something to eat. He was ready for both, but instead the old fellow rummaged around in an old bureau until he found a yellowing sheet of paper.

'Come here, one o' you!' he said imperiously. As he was closest, Ben went up to Constable Ballard, who handed him the sheet of paper, saying, 'read them words out loud now!'

The young man took the document and then, speaking in a clear and determined voice, read out, 'I, Ben Drake, do solemnly swear that I will perform with fidelity the duties of the office which I am about to assume. I do solemnly swear to support the constitution of the United States and to faithfully perform the duties of the office of deputy constable for the Territory of New Mexico. I further swear that I have not promised or given, nor will I give any fee, gift, gratuity, or reward for this office or for aid in procuring this office; that I will not take any fee, gift, or bribe, or gratuity for returning any person as a juror or for making any false return of any process, and that I will faithfully execute the office of constable to the best of my knowledge and ability, agreeably to law.'

After he had finished, Ballard said, 'Well, boy, you're now a duly appointed deputy. You others, come now and read this out, one by one.'

When all four of them had repeated the formula, the old constable ferreted about further in a drawer of the bureau and came up with four tarnished badges, each in the form of a six-pointed star.

'There now, they're all I got. Pat, you can deputize those other men o' whom you spoke.' Ballard led them outside again and settled himself back into his rocker. 'There now, I'm tired out with all them official duties. I reckon I'll be taking a little snooze. Good luck with your huntin'!'

After they had mounted up and left Fiddler's Creek, Sweeney said to Tim Johnson and Horse, 'You two ride on ahead for a spell. I want a few private words with young Ben here.'

Johnson and Horse exchanged puzzled glances, but did as they had been bid. When once they were out of earshot, Sweeney said, 'I didn't hear your last name 'til a few minutes since. Unless it's a rare coincidence, I'm guessing that you are that same Ben Drake whose pa was Clarence Drake. Used to live near Mason. That right?'

'I was raised in Mason County,' said Ben, 'left when I was seven years of age.'

'After your pa was lynched?'

'Yes, sir. You know about that?'

'It was only ten or eleven years ago. Most everybody in Mason knows about it.'

'Could you tell me what happened? I'd sure like to know.'

'It was a bad business, son. But here's how it went. I figure you got a right to know.'

CHAPTER 5

In the early spring of 1866, Clarence Drake and his wife, together with their five-year-old son, fetched up in the little town of Mason. The end of the Great War between the States had left Drake with no money and few skills; other than the ability to shoot straight and ride hard. There was, unfortunately, no shortage of men with just those talents, so Clarence Drake had taken up an invitation from a man he'd met during the war to come and help run a ranch. He knew a little about cattle, having grown up on a ranch himself.

Clarence Drake's wife, Abigail, came from a fairly well-to-do family and they provided funds enough to acquire a little house on the outskirts of Mason.

For the next two years, everything went well with the Drake family. Clarence was a hard worker and got on well with Pat Sweeney, the man who had invited him to come to Mason. From the beginning, Drake's position was not that of hired hand, but rather of a very junior partner in the business that Sweeney had established. There was one fly in the ointment and that was a neighbouring rancher called Angus McBride. By some means, it had been suggested that bribery was involved; McBride had managed to swing a contract from the army to supply them with beef. This was the beginning of some big business, although this first contract was a relatively modest one.

Seeing Clarence Drake as something of an asset, McBride visited him at his home one night in the spring of 1868 and offered him a strong cash inducement to change sides and to come and work for McBride's outfit. When he refused, Angus McBride grew angry and was so intemperate in his speech that Drake was obliged to turn him out of the house; for which McBride never forgave him.

It was an open question at that time which of the two men, Angus McBride or Patrick Sweeney, would become the biggest and most influential rancher in Mason County. Two things tipped the balance in McBride's favour. One of these was winning that first contract with the army, the other was branching out into dry goods. McBride's enterprise in opening a store in Mason took Sweeney by surprise and so did the army contract. Sweeney had tendered for that same contract and was astounded that McBride was able to undercut the prices that Sweeney had himself quoted.

Together, Sweeney and Drake planned a counter gambit to McBride: the importation of cheap steers from outside the county and then tendering at rock-bottom prices for a contract of their own to supply the army with meat. Drake went south to collect the steers and as he was returning to Mason, disaster struck.

On the early evening of 15th June, 1868, Clarence Drake and two men who worked for him and Sweeney were bringing twenty head of cattle towards Mason. These few steers were just a sample of what could be available from this source on a regular basis. They looked pretty good to Drake, healthy and well nourished, but he knew that Pat Sweeney would want to see some for himself before he entered into any binding arrangement with those who were offering to do business with them. Fifteen miles from town, the three men and their steers were met by a posse of men led by Angus McBride.

At first, Drake was amused, rather than alarmed, by the presumption shown in trying to impede their progress in the highway like that. He said to McBride, 'What's afoot? You bushwhacking us or something?

'I'm looking into a case of stock theft,' replied McBride. 'Got reason to suppose you've stolen some of my cattle.'

'You're crazy as a coot, McBride,' laughed Clarence Drake, 'now just let me pass, you hear what I tell you?'

'Not 'til my boys have looked at those steers you got. Make a move and you'll be shot down.'

Three of McBride's men rode forwards. They were cradling scatterguns in their arms, aimed in the general direction of Drake and the other two men. They were heavily outnumbered and outgunned, so at least for the time being, Drake thought that it was the smart move to remain silent and see what developed.

One of McBride's men called out, 'Yeah, it's like we suspicioned, boss. This'un's one o' ours.'

'Don't be a damned fool,' said Drake, 'I bought these steers over the county line. There's not a chance in hell that any of 'em belong to you.'

Then things happened very fast. One of Sweeney's men decided that he didn't like the way things were tending, so he spurred on his horse and went for his pistol at the same time. His partner, fearing perhaps that he was on the point of being lynched and preferring to die on his own terms, also pulled his pistol and began firing at McBride's men, who returned fire at once. Clarence Drake was taken quite aback by this turn of events and just sat there, gaping at what was happening around him. As the echoes of the shooting died away, two men rode up and deprived Drake of his weapon.

Both of the men that Drake had been riding alongside for the last couple of days were dead, and he said in amazement to Angus McBride, 'You gone too far this time, McBride. You'll hang for this day's work.'

'I don't think so,' said the other man confidently, 'I'd say the boot's on the other foot, Drake.'

It was only then that Clarence Drake fully realized the deadly peril in which he was situated. There was

THE VINDICATORS

no official law in Mason at that time; only a vigilance committee. Unofficial hangings were by no means an uncommon occurrence in the county. Still, thought Drake, once they examine the brands on these cattle properly, folks will see that they aren't McBride's property. He had underestimated the cunning of the man who now encompassed his death. McBride had no intention of letting anybody look closely at the actual cattle which Drake had been accompanying when stopped.

He said, 'All right, you men know what you got to do. It's as clear a case of rustling as ever I saw. Hang him!'

'You can't,' cried Drake, in sudden terror. 'I can show you the bill of sale for those steers, look here.'

He delved into his pocket and produced a crumpled piece of paper. One of the men took this from him and handed it to Angus McBride, who put it in his own pocket without looking at it.

'Hang him!' he said again.

A week later, nobody in Mason feeling strong enough or certain enough of the facts to contradict McBride's account of the incident to do anything about Clarence Drake's death, Patrick Sweeney put the dead man's wife and son on to a stage heading north and within a month, everybody but him had forgotten about the business.

'And that's how it was,' said Sweeney to the young man riding at his side. 'Maybe I should have done more. I sure felt guilty about your pa's death, but what's done is written. Can't be changed now.'

'So my pa wasn't a rustler? You're certain-sure 'bout that?'

'Never been surer about anything in my life. He was no more a rustler than I am. I'm more than half of the opinion that McBride himself is rustling. You ever notice how folk up to no good are often quick off the mark to accuse others of the very thing they're guilty of themselves?'

But Ben Drake wasn't listening any more to Sweeney. His heart felt that light that he was almost giddy with it. It was as though for most of his life he'd been living half in some dark shadow, and now this had lifted and he was bathed in golden sunlight. He felt an almost physical sense of well-being and exhilaration. I guess, he thought to himself, you could say that I have vindicated my father now.

Sweeney signalled the other two lads that they could rejoin them. Johnson and Horse gave Ben odd looks; they looked like they were absolutely dying to know what this private talk had been about. Ben, for his part, wasn't about to enlighten them. He felt that if ever a subject had been his own, personal business, then the death of his father must surely belong in that category.

'What are we going to do now, Mr Sweeney?' asked Tim Johnson. 'Are we going back to your ranch?'

'Not yet awhiles, son. First off is where we need to acquire warrants for those scoundrels who slayed your boss. A constable can't issue such, they need to be sworn out by a court or a justice. I know a justice of the peace who lives not far from here. It's on the road back home. We coulda called in before visiting Sam Ballard, but I wanted to make sure that we were all deputies first. Makes his job of issuing the warrants more legal and above board.'

'What happens then, sir?' asked Horse.

'What happens next? Why, we go and arrest Angus McBride and his friends. That's if you boys are game?'

The three youngsters assured Sweeney that they were game enough for the job. He laughed and said, 'Well then, let's get those warrants and then go home and collect your friends. The more guns on our side of the road, the better.'

The ride back towards Mason was pleasant and relaxed, despite the grim nature of their journey. The sun was shining and all around them were the beautiful sights and sounds of nature.

Now that the pleasure of discovering for sure that his pa had been wrongfully lynched had sunk in, Ben was starting to wonder what he ought to do next. Should he just return to his grandparents' home with the account that Mr Sweeney had furnished him? This was not an enticing prospect, to say the least of it. He and his grandfather didn't precisely see eye to eye on a whole heap of different subjects and before Ben had left to come to Mason, things had been pretty fraught between them. It was certainly the case that he had enjoyed life more in the last month than in the whole of the preceding year or more.

Then again, there was the circumstance of Chuck Taylor's murder, which was really just lynching under

69

another name. In the few brief weeks that he had known Mr Taylor, he had been most favourably impressed with the man. It would seem kind of churlish to run out now, when all the others were dead set on bringing Taylor's murderer to justice. Also, having set out to vindicate one man's name from a false charge of lynching, did he not have some kind of obligation to help out in another case of the same kind?

It is impossible to say which of these various factors weighed most heavily when Ben Drake was weighing up the options available to him. Without doubt, he was not at all eager to rejoin his grandparents' establishment. Not only that, he was overflowing with relief about sorting out the accusation which had hung over his pa's memory for most of his young life. Whatever the precise reasons, by the time that the four of them had reached the justice of the peace's home, Ben Drake had decided to throw in his lot with those seeking justice for Chuck Taylor.

Justice of the Peace Linton Cathcart appeared to be another old friend of Sweeney's. He greeted the rancher even more effusively than Sam Ballard had done and in more robust terms.

'Sweeney, you old bastard,' he said, when he opened the door of his home, 'what stone have you been hiding under? Come in and set yourself down. Who are these young fellows? Illegitimate sons of yours?'

Sweeney laughed. 'Hallo, Cathcart. It's business, not pleasure. I want to lay information against a set of killers and hope as you'll issue warrants for their arrest. We've all been deputized.'

For all that Linton Cathcart was an old and intimate friend of Pat Sweeney's, he asked many questions about the status of the four men; wanting to assure himself before he took a single step that the whole thing was open and above board. Once he was satisfied that they really were deputy constables, he went over to his desk and wrote out a number of warrants. Angus McBride and his sons were no problem, but when it came to the *vaqueros*, they soon hit a difficulty.

'I'm not giving out blank warrants, authorizing you to take into custody any Mexican that crosses your path,' warned Cathcart. 'I'm only doing this by names.'

'His foreman's called Francis Xavier,' said Horse.

'So he is,' agreed Sweeney, 'There now, that's a name.'

When he'd written out the four warrants, three for the McBrides and one for their foreman, Cathcart said, 'What about that sheriff? You want I should do a warrant for him too, on a charge of murder?'

'Lord, no,' said Sweeney, 'I don't want to start a war. It's going to be tricky enough apprehending McBride, without mounting an assault on the Mason County sheriff. If we're not careful, we'll draw the army into the game. I hope to achieve this without a lot of shooting.'

'You'll be lucky!' declared Cathcart. 'You think as Angus McBride'll consent to being led off quietly into captivity? I woulda thought you knew him better than that.'

As Sweeney and the three youths approached Mason, Sweeney said to his young companions, 'I don't want any of you to go boasting around town about any of this, you hear what I tell you? We'll rest up tonight at my place and then tomorrow morning, we'll go after McBride. This has been a long time coming, and I'm much to blame for not taking some strong action about that man years ago. It could have saved blood being spilled.'

Now, Patrick Sweeney was a good man, but he was not as fatherly a person as Chuck Taylor had been. Taylor loved and understood the boys who worked for him in a way that Sweeney did not. For Sweeney, it was enough that he had told three of those twenty-one young men that he didn't want them to go running off at the mouth in town about the pro-jected action against the McBrides and their foreman. He took it for granted that this was all that was needed. Taylor would have spoken to each of those youths in turn and impressed upon every one of them, most forcibly, what he expected.

As the sun swooped towards the horizon that evening, five men went trotting off towards town. Tim Johnson was a real hot-head and he was just itching to take Angus McBride off to gaol or worse for what he had done to Mr Taylor. Johnson was an orphan and his dead boss was the only man whom Johnson had ever respected or thought might be able to understand him. He was more grieved about

Taylor's death than any of the others were. Being sworn in as a deputy had gone to Tim Johnson's head and he was more than half convinced that his new-found status put him on about the same level as Sheriff Palmer.

The Silver Dollar was doing a roaring trade that night. The atmosphere of the saloon was enough to make men feel more tipsy than was warranted by the amount of liquor they had taken. Johnson and his four friends had a few drinks, all the while looking around for anybody from Angus McBride's outfit. No matter what the justice had said, Johnson had his own views on men getting away with murder, just because nobody knew their name. Inevitably, after a couple of shots of whiskey, Tim Johnson began proclaiming what he intended to do to those damned McBrides.

'You fellows don't know shit!' he announced loudly and aggressively. 'All these years an' you been letting' that bastard cow's son get away with murder. Murder, I tell you!'

'Hey, Tim,' said one of the others, 'I reckon we should keep it down a mite.'

'The hell with that,' replied Johnson forcefully. 'Days when folk had to pussyfoot round that McBride are long past.' He turned to the rest of the clientele of The Silver Dollar and announced, 'The day of judgement is approaching, folks. Day when that bastard McBride is goin' to be brought down.'

By happy chance, there were none of McBride's men in the saloon that night. It was busy up at

McBride's ranch and there was no time for drinking that day. Nobody knew this, though, and after Tim Johnson had been mouthing off for a spell, one of the other drinkers slipped out and went down the street to tip the wink to Joe Palmer that there could be trouble brewing.

Palmer was wondering seriously if the game he was in was playing any more. Not only had he found himself being present when a cold-blooded murder had been committed, but he had noticed over the last week or so that Angus McBride was adopting an openly contemptuous air towards him as though the gloves were off and it was acknowledged that he was, and always had been, just another of those employed by McBride; no different from one of his damned *vaqueros*. Until recently, the fiction had always been maintained that no matter what the circumstances of Palmer's elevation to the post of sheriff, he was a free and independent peace officer. Just lately, Angus McBride seemed to be finding it too much of an effort to keep up this pretence.

Now, although Joe Palmer didn't want to think of himself as being just McBride's personal protector or guardian, he also knew that if anything did happen to the old man, then he, Palmer, would find himself out on a very long limb. He had a strong motive for seeing that Angus McBride remained in a strong and influential position in Mason County, his own livelihood depending upon this. So it was that when he heard that one of the late Chuck Taylor's men was in The Silver Dollar, shouting the odds, the sheriff thought that he ought to go and quieten things down a little before everybody was sorry.

Back in the saloon, Tim Johnson was becoming ever more lively and contentious. His friends, none of whom had gone with him to Fiddler's Creek and were therefore most assuredly not deputies in their own right, were becoming distinctly uneasy at the way things were tending. Johnson alone was heeled and if trouble erupted, then the other four men would be defenceless. If it came to that, Johnson himself was no great shakes with a pistol.

Instead of the band of heavily armed *vaqueros* that they were secretly dreading, in walked that most unassuming and generally harmless of individuals, Sheriff Joe Palmer. Until the incident when their boss was murdered, most of Taylor's men regarded Joe Palmer as being innocuous. He turned a blind eye in general to drunkenness, never made much of himself and seemed to wish to avoid trouble, rather than court it. He was widely viewed as being beholden to Angus McBride, but then the same could be said about many others in Mason.

After another whiskey, Johnson was becoming even more specific about Angus McBride and what was waiting for him in the not too distant future. He said, 'And another thing you men mightn't know is this. I'm a deputy now myself! What d'you all say to that, hey?'

In truth, they said nothing at all to that, because all they had come to The Silver Dollar for was a quiet drink. There wasn't one of them who wished to get mixed up in somebody else's range war. It was at this moment that Joe Palmer entered the saloon and went up to Johnson. Palmer might have been a weak and in some ways corrupt man, but he was very far from being a coward. In the present instance, he was as keen to save this rash young man from the consequences of his intoxication as he was anything else. He said, 'Son, I woulda thought you had about enough to drink now. Why'nt you get yourself home to your friends?'

This was fairly spoken and the patrons of The Silver Dollar were, to a man, in agreement with the sheriff. The young man was being a nuisance and disturbing all the other drinkers. Tim Johnson, though, saw the case differently. He said, 'Well, look here. If it ain't the man who killed Chuck Taylor. You can't touch me, Palmer. We're cut from the same length o' cloth now. I'm a lawman too.'

'Nobody wants an argument with you,' said Palmer quietly. 'Just you get yourself home and there's no harm done.' He turned to the other four boys and said, 'You fellows would be doin' your partner a kindness, were you to take him off now. Otherwise, there's apt to be unpleasantness.'

'Come on, man,' one of the young men said to Johnson, uneasily, 'let's dig up. We got an early start in the morning, you 'member?'

Slowly and deliberately, Tim Johnson stepped clear of his friends and said clearly, 'This here's one of those who shot down the best man as ever walked the earth. He ain't fit to lick Mr Taylor's boots and yet

there he stands. The man as laid Taylor in his grave.'
Then he leaned forward and spat in Sheriff Palmer's
face, before going for his gun.

CHAPTER 6

By all the conventions prevailing at that time, Joe Palmer would have been well within his rights to shoot down the young man in front of him, on the spot. Johnson had gone for his weapon in the presence of a dozen witnesses and nobody would blame the sheriff for pulling his own piece and firing first. But Tim Johnson was not sober and had never drawn a gun in a real, life-and-death situation before. The hammer caught on his belt as he drew and while he was fumbling to free it, Joe Palmer took pity on the boy and knew that it would be sheer murder to shoot him at that moment. Instead, he pulled his own gun out and smashed it into the side of Johnson's head. The two-pound chunk of steel was enough to settle the matter for the time being, because it had the effect of sending young Tim Johnson crashing to the floor, knocked out by the blow.

The sheriff might not have been the most popular man in Mason, but the men drinking in The Silver Dollar that night were appreciative of the way that he had settled a tricky problem without resorting to bloodshed. They were particularly impressed when they saw Palmer take out a handkerchief and wipe away the spittle from his face. Few of them would have been forgiving enough to ignore such a deadly insult as that and the sheriff's stock rose accordingly.

'You fellows,' said Palmer to the frightened-looking youngsters who had been standing next to Johnson, 'why don't you get yourselves off and leave your friend here. He'll come to no harm. I just aim to put him in the cell in my office, 'til he sobers up.'

The four young men needed no second bidding and left the saloon at once. When they had gone, the sheriff said, 'Can one of you men lend a hand here? I want to carry this young fool down the street to my office. I fear to pick him up unaided, for fear of doing my back a mischief.'

There were several volunteers and in a short time, Tim Johnson was securely lodged in the single cell which occupied the back portion of Palmer's office. Before they left, one of the men said to Palmer, 'You handled that right well, Sheriff. You'd have been in your rights to shoot that kid.'

'Ah, he's only a boy. Like as not, he'll sober up and by the morning he'll be apologizing to me.'

By the time the four remaining members of the party which had set out from Pat Sweeney's ranch a few hours earlier got home, it was nearly midnight. Sweeney and his men had gone to bed and only Chuck Taylor's young workers were sitting round a little fire and talking about the next stage in bringing

Angus McBride to justice.

Because he was still elated at having only that day learned for sure that there was no substance in the accusations levelled against his father which had led to his being lynched, Ben Drake said little during these conversations. This gave some of the others the impression that he was a little lukewarm on the subject of avenging Mr Taylor's death. Nothing could have been further from the truth. The reality was that Ben had an even stronger motive than any of those others for wanting to settle accounts with Angus McBride. He had lost his real father due to the man's lies and crooked dealings. None of the others knew this, though, so they had decided that because the new fellow wasn't joining in their extravagant protestations of loyalty to the memory of their boss, he wasn't really that fussed about going after McBride.

When they heard the rumble of hoof beats, the boys seated around the fire assumed that Tim Johnson and the others were returning from town. Only four riders arrived, though, leading a riderless horse.

'Where's Tim?' asked somebody.

'Town gaol, most likely,' was the surprising reply.

Once the story had been told, there were various exclamations about the unfairness of it all and the fact that Joe Palmer was no more than McBride's lapdog. Ben Drake kept his own counsel during this talk, having already decided what he himself would be doing about this. After the others had exhausted the topic and were more or less resigned, despite all the big talk, to leaving Tim Johnson in the cell overnight, Ben said quietly, 'Who'll come with me to free Tim from the gaol?'

There was a dead silence. The idea that they could really march into town like that and take such a hazardous action had never really crossed anybody's mind until Ben put the notion into words and spoke them out loud. He said again, 'Who'll help me? Tim Johnson is a duly authorized peace officer. Sheriff's got no business at all locking him up in that way. A bunch of us could go up there this very night and bust him out.'

'You mean fight the sheriff?'

'Maybe,' said Ben, 'but it might not come to that. Does Sheriff Palmer sleep over his office?'

'No,' said another of the young men, slowly, 'him an' his wife live out on the edge of town. A fair pace from the office.'

'Tell me now,' said Ben, 'what's this office of his like? How secure is this cell?'

It turned out that the cell at the back of Sheriff Palmer's office was anything but secure. There had already been one break-out from it in the past, when the blacksmith had been locked up for the night. He had managed to force apart two of the bars in the window and climb out. Since that time, the window had been strengthened and now consisted of a strong lattice of steel bars.

Ben thought about this and then said, 'The bars may be strong enough and I daresay they're fixed

81

firmly enough to the frame of the window, but I wonder how that's fixed to the wall?'

'How d'you mean?' asked somebody.

'Well, I've seen a house being built. Window frames are made of wood, right? They're only secured to the brick walls by a nail or two and a smear of mortar. How'd it be if we took a rope with us and fixed it to the bars of this window? Think a horse might pull it out altogether, rip it from the wall?'

'It might,' said one of the boys, admiringly. 'It just might!'

Nobody thought that it was a good idea to awaken Mr Sweeney. This was less out of consideration for the man and a desire to avoid disturbing his slumbers, than because they were all of them aware that Sweeney might forbid an expedition of this sort. Twenty young men riding down on Mason at this time of night might be expected to invite questions. At the very least, it was a circumstance which might later be remembered by somebody living in the town. It was accordingly thought wise if only three of them went to town to try their luck at the rescue. Ben was one, since it had been his idea. Horse was an obvious choice for another, because of his strength. Young Ralph Moore was chosen as the third, because he was desperately keen to put one over on Sheriff Palmer since the murder of his boss. They took Johnson's horse along with them.

The streets of Mason were as quiet and dark as the middle of the prairie at that time of night. On the one hand, thought Ben, this was good. It meant that with a little luck, nobody would mark their presence that night. On the other hand, it mean that if they made any noise while freeing their friend from gaol, it would most likely draw attention to them and lead to the Lord knew what complications.

Although the sheriff's office was right on Main Street, in the most prominent location imaginable, the cell was at the back and the single window faced an empty lot. There were no lights on, either in the office or in any of the neighbouring buildings. In fact, glancing up and down the street, Ben Drake couldn't see a single glimmer of lamplight anywhere.

'Looks promising!' he said to the young men at his side. 'What say we dismount and lead our horses round the back of the office?'

When they were round back of the office, Ben went up to the window, which was about five feet from the ground, and hissed in a low voice, 'Tim, you in there?'

'Yeah, sure I'm here. Who's that?'

'It's me, Ben Drake. We've come to set you loose.'

There was a long silence, until Ben began to be worried that the other man had fallen asleep or something. He said, 'Tim, you still there, man?'

'Yeah, course I am,' said the other, with a slight catch in his voice. It sounded as though, although of course it was quite impossible, that the young man in the cell was choking back tears. Ben thought that it might be tactful to take no notice of this and said, 'Listen, we're going to pass a length of rope through the bars. Can you push it back again? Well, do that a few times and make sure as the rope is firmly fixed to them bars.'

When the rope had been securely lashed to the bars of the little window, the other end was made fast to the saddle and bridle of Ben's horse, in an impro-vised harness.

When this had been done, he said to the other two, 'Well, let's do this. Listen, you boys had best have Tim's horse there ready and waiting. You can ride it up to the window if this works and he can climb straight on to it.'

With that, Ben mounted up and got his horse moving. At first, nothing happened and he began to fear that the window was too well attached to the fabric of the building, but then there was an unearthly, metallic screeching, which must have been audible for half a mile or more, and Ben's horse lurched suddenly forwards. Nearby, a dog began barking at the noise that they had made and across the lot, there was a flicker of light as somebody lit a lamp. It was time to go.

When he turned in the saddle, Ben saw that Tim Johnson had scrambled out of the window and was already mounted on his horse. Ben untied the rope from his own horse and tossed it to the ground. There was nothing to distinguish that length of rope from any other.

'Let's head out!' he said to the others.

On the way back to Sweeney's ranch, Tim Johnson would not leave Ben's side. He had learned from the others that it had been Ben's idea alone to come and rescue him, and that nobody else had even thought of such a thing.

He said to Ben, 'I ain't ever goin' to forget this. Not ever, in the whole course o' my life. I swear it.'

'Hey, it's nothing,' said Ben, embarrassed, 'it's nothing at all.'

'It's something,' said Tim. From that night onwards, it seemed to Ben that some part of the dog-like devotion which Tim Johnson had felt for Chuck Taylor was transferred to him. He'd never thought that Tim was all that keen on him, but from then on in, the fellow was always at his elbow, just waiting to be of use.

When Sweeney heard the next day what had happened, the boys thought that he'd be furious, but he just shook his head despairingly and said, 'You men'll be the death of me.'

Ben said, 'When do we go after Angus McBride, sir?'

'Not this day, if you'll all be guided by me. He's like to be on edge right now. I'm strongly of the opinion that we should let things cool off a little.'

'For how long?' asked Ben, acting naturally as the spokesman for the others.

Sweeney gave him an odd look and said, 'Only a day or two. No more. What I suggest is that you men go back to Chuck Taylor's ranch today and then spend the night there. I make no doubt that there's plenty of food for you all about the place. You may as well help yourselves to aught that you need, you being the nearest thing Taylor had to kith and kin.

There's animals need tending to, apart from any other consideration. I'll ride over tomorrow and we'll lay our plans then.'

So definite did Pat Sweeney appear to be about this plan, that none of the youngsters had the courage to gainsay him. They saddled up and left within a half-hour. None of them ever saw Sweeney alive again. Whether he had some premonition about this or if it was just because having discovered that Ben was the son of an old friend, just before they left, Sweeney went to Ben and handed him a sheaf of papers, saying, 'You best take charge of these.'

Ben looked at him inquiringly and Pat Sweeney told him, 'These here are the warrants for those men. You keep 'em safe now.'

There was a whole heap of work to be done when they got back to the Taylor spread, and Sweeney had been right about animals needing to be looked after. Some would certainly not have made it if they hadn't come back today to see to them. It felt wrong, but two of them went into the big house and found Taylor's keys there. As Sweeney had said, Chuck Taylor had had no other kin and they might as well try and keep things running, now that he was gone. For that, they would need the money which he kept locked away in his house.

It was a hard day's work for them all and when evening came, they were about ready for an early night. They retired to the cabins and by eleven were all asleep.

It was Ralph Moore who woke Ben up in the early

hours of the morning. He had gone outside to make water and seen an eerie glow in the sky, over to the east. At first, he had thought that it might be later than he realized and that this was the first light of dawn. Then he saw that the ruddy light was flickering and knew that it was flames.

It was something of a mystery to Ben why it should have been to him that Ralph carried this news. Did he but know it, his determination to free Tim Johnson from the sheriff's office the night before had raised his status greatly among the other youngsters. Some of them were looking upon him almost as a leader.

'Show me, Ralph,' said Ben, as he climbed out of the bunk. 'Wait 'til I get on my boots.'

As soon as he was outside, it was plain that there was a fire raging somewhere, over in the east. With a sinking heart, Ben knew that the ominous light was coming from pretty much the same direction as Sweeney's spread. He toyed with the idea of waking the others, but then decided against it. It would have been madness for them to go chasing off in the middle of the night to investigate this. Better by far to wait until morning.

He said to Ralph, 'You did well to tell me about this. You get back to sleep now and we'll see what's what when dawn comes.'

The next day, Ben waited until everybody was awake before talking about what had been seen in the night.

'What d'you make of it?' asked somebody.

87

'I'd say it means mischief of some sort or another,' he replied. 'I'd take oath that somebody raised a fire on Mr Sweeney's property last night. I vote we get over there right soon and see what we can do to help.'

It took a little while for them all to get ready, break their fast and so on, but it wasn't long after eight when they set off to see what might have happened at the Sweeney ranch. Most of them were thinking in terms of rick-burning or something of that nature. They were quite unprepared for what greeted them.

Facing Patrick Sweeney's house was a substantial barn, with a hayloft. This was now a charred ruin. The air was sharp with the tang of burned wood; you could smell it a good half-mile before reaching the scene of the fire. Ben was relieved to see that it was only a barn and not Sweeney's house which had been fired. He had had a terrible feeling when he saw that glow in the sky and had expected something worse than merely a fired barn. Then he caught sight, as they approached the yard in front of the house, of a knot of men. They were not busying themselves with tidying up after the fire or doing anything much, other than standing around, looking down at something which lay on the ground. As they came nearer, it was obvious that this was a body and Ben didn't need to go any further to know that it was that of Patrick Sweeney.

What had happened was brutally simple. Somebody had set fire to the barn in the middle of the night. Being so close to the house, it was a certainty that

Patrick Sweeney would have seen the flames and then come out; either to investigate the blaze or to help with extinguishing it. Someone had been waiting with a rifle, off to the side of the house a little way, possibly behind the low stone wall which ran alongside the yard. As soon as Sweeney had come running from the house, he had been silhouetted by the blazing barn and the hidden gunman had fired just a single shot, killing him immediately. It was, it had to be admitted, a brilliantly planned assassination.

It looked as though, for Angus McBride, the gloves were well and truly off. He had put up, grudgingly, with competition in the cattle business for better than ten years, but the opening of the new store had acted as a catalyst and prompted him to settle all outstanding business. Having disposed of Chuck Taylor, he had seemingly thought that taking a shot at Sweeney under the cover of darkness would be a smart move. Perhaps he was right, because now the only other person in the district, probably the entire county, who would stand up against the McBrides, was gone.

Sweeney's men didn't look over-pleased to see the posse of youngsters. They were calculating that with Pat Sweeney dead and gone, they would all be out of jobs and homes. Since the death had been precipitated by the trouble between Taylor and McBride, they tended to blame his former employees for matters reaching such a point. One of them said as much, when the young men dismounted and came over to view the body.

He said, 'You men are the cause of this here. Weren't for you, none of this woulda happened. You're not welcome here.'

The others standing round their boss's body said nothing but stared balefully at the young men, until they felt it best to get back on their horses and ride off again.

As they trotted back to Chuck Taylor's ranch, Ben remarked to Tim Johnson, 'That's a facer and no mistake.'

'Yeah, I kind o' liked that Mr Sweeney,' said Johnson. 'D'you really think he was killed 'cause of us?'

'No, I wouldn't have thought so. I think as that Angus McBride's just thought it's time to clear up all his outstanding problems and deal with everything at once. He woulda killed Mr Sweeney, even if he hadn't helped us.'

'What do you say we should do now? I can't live with that bastard McBride getting away with murdering Mr Taylor. You still game for going after him?'

Ben Drake turned in surprise and said, ' 'Course I'm going after him. I figured you might want to as well, but I don't know 'bout some of the others.'

'Half o' them'll cut and run,' predicted Johnson gloomily. 'I'd be right taken aback if we end up with more'n a dozen of us.'

'That's enough to do the job,' said Ben, with a new-found confidence.

By the time they got back to the Taylor place, the twenty-one riders had split up into small groups, discussing what had chanced that day and working out the best course of action for the future. There were two main motives at work. Those who had folks or friends they could go and stay with, or who had not worked very long for Chuck Taylor were in favour of leaving at once and avoiding any further danger. Those, on the other hand, like Tim Johnson, who had no family or friends apart from those he had made while with Taylor, were still hot for vengeance against the men who had killed him. A cynical observer might have remarked that this party, about half the men in total, were only keen on staying put in New Mexico because they had nowhere else to go.

When they had returned, Johnson suggested, somewhat aggressively, a show of hands to indicate who wanted to pursue the vendetta and who just wanted, as he put it, 'to cut and run'. Precisely as he had prophesied, ten of the youngsters were in favour of going at once. There was nothing more to be said, and those who wanted to leave collected their gear from the bunkhouses and departed that very morning. There remained Ben Drake, Tim Johnson, Ralph Moore, Horse and seven others.

As though he were a kid starting a secret society in the schoolyard, Tim Johnson said, 'Hey, we need to have a name for our outfit. What's you fellows say to the Revengers?'

Ben laughed good-naturedly. He said, 'Tell you what, I have the perfect name. What about the Vindicators?'

'What in hell does that mean?' asked Ralph.

91

Ben explained the meaning of the word to them, touching as it did upon restoring a man's good name and reputation. They all agreed that it was a most apposite title for what they planned; which was nothing less than the vindication of Chuck Taylor's name from the slur of being a rustler.

Johnson at once gave way and so it was that this group of eleven young men, ranging in age between eighteen and twenty-three, came to call themselves, the Vindicators.

CHAPTER 7

There was enough food stored at the ranch to keep the eleven of them going for a time and they also overcame their scruples about entering the big house. At first, it seemed like robbing the dead, but if they were to survive and restore Chuck Taylor's good name, then they would surely need money to do so. It was accordingly agreed that they would use the cash which they found in the house, but strictly for living expenses. Not a cent was to be spent on alcohol, gambling or any foolishness of that sort.

Now, a curious circumstance was that Ben Drake hadn't mentioned to a single one of the others that he had his own, entirely personal reasons for being part of their band. The other men were all touched that somebody who had known Mr Taylor for such a short time would nevertheless be prepared to give up everything to see his death avenged and his reputation preserved. They had not the least notion that Ben was determined to see Angus McBride punished for his role in the killing of Clarence Drake all those years ago. The others knew that he, unlike them, had a family home to which he could return at any time; which, to them, had the effect of making his devotion to this cause even more praiseworthy.

A posse of eleven armed men cannot just go riding around the countryside, looking for victims, without attracting attention. It was true that three of them had been legally deputized and that they had warrants for the men they were looking for, but even so, it would invite trouble. The decision was made therefore to try and find when and where the men that they were hunting would be found alone. Nobody wanted to end up in a big gun battle if it could possibly be avoided. This was particularly the case with Ben Drake, whose experience with firearms was limited to using a scattergun when out hunting fowl with his grandfather.

Ralph Moore was the youngest and by far and away most harmless-looking of their band, so he was sent to town to hang round and try to get some idea of where they could find any of their targets in the right circumstances. While Ralph was gone, the others thought it might be time to break out some weapons and prepare for action.

Chuck Taylor had been something of a collector of firearms. He had formerly been an officer in the Confederate army and this had given him an interest in weaponry. A rack in the storeroom attached to the kitchen contained four rifles and a matching pair of fowling pieces. There were also eight pistols of various types about the house. Not only this, but they also found in a spare room various cavalry swords and wicked-looking Bowie knives.

'Why,' exclaimed one of the youngsters, 'this house is a regular armoury!'

Much as he would have liked to start toting a pistol or carrying a rifle around, Ben knew that it would be mere swagger and bravado to do so. Worse than that, it would likely get him killed. Anybody seeing him with a gun at his hip could challenge him to a duel over any fancied slight; with inevitably deadly consequences for him. He hardly had time to learn to shoot a pistol at this stage of the proceedings. The fowling pieces, though, were something else again. He picked one up and hefted it in his hand.

The scattergun was a beautiful piece of craftsmanship. The stock was walnut; polished and varnished until it was as smooth as silk. The twin hammers were fashioned like tiny dolphins and the twin barrels were etched with a design of vine leaves and fruit.

'If nobody else wants it,' said Ben, 'I'll take this.'

'A shotgun?' said Tim in amazement. 'With them rifles to choose from? Sure, you can have it. I'm damned sure nobody else'll want to cart around such a big thing as that.'

'Yes, but you see it's not going to be so big, not when I've finished with it.'

'What d'you mean?'

'Well, if we're allowed to take this stuff, then I reckon nobody'll object if I adapt it a little.'

It seemed a shame to mutilate such a fine weapon, but it would have been an ungainly thing to try and cart around on horseback. He took the scattergun to the nearby shed, where there was a selection of tools, including various saws. Choosing one with a narrow blade, Ben cut a foot and a half from the two barrels. Then he turned his attention to the stock, removing six inches or so. He was left with a handy weapon which could be carried easily over his shoulder, when once he had fitted a sling to it.

Tim Johnson and the others were faintly aghast when they saw how Ben had treated the scattergun. But in the end, they realized that it was no worse than their own actions in helping themselves to the guns and ammunition. After all, none of this stuff belonged to anybody in particular as they could see. The old school chant of 'finders keepers, losers weepers' was probably at the back of their minds.

When he had taken a length of leather and attached it to the scattergun, Ben had a perfectly serviceable weapon which could be carried around comfortably. He loaded it and then slipped percussion caps under the nipples. He'd an idea that it wouldn't be long before he had occasion to use the thing.

In town, Ralph had an unexpected stroke of luck. News of Pat Sweeney's killing had not yet reached Mason so everybody was as relaxed and cheerful as you like. The first place that Ralph Moore visited was McBride's grand store, and it was there that he overheard the conversation which lit the fuse, triggering the bloody events of the next couple of weeks.

'Saw that fellow of McBride's yestereve,' said a

man to his companion. They were both of them farmers, by the look of it; probably in the store to buy seed or some agricultural implement or other. 'Says his boss wants him to go up to Santa Fe today. There's something brewing, I don't rightly mind what.'

'You mean that one as has a name sounds like some saint or other?'

'Yeah, that's him. Francis something. Funny thing for a greaser to be a callin' hisself.'

'Well,' said the other man, 'he ain't yet gone to Santa Fe. Saw him proppin' up the bar of The Silver Dollar just a quarter-hour since.'

'There's some as start early in the day!'

At once, Ralph left the store and walked briskly down Main Street to The Silver Dollar. He was so fresh-faced and young-looking, that he had never yet been served in the saloon. Sometimes, he'd been thrown out, on the grounds that they didn't like to see minors hanging round the place. This was irksome; specially since he was the same age as Ben Drake. Still, there it was. A swift glance over the top of the batwing doors was enough to confirm that the man known as Francis Xavier was still at the bar. He was talking to two or three other men, who also looked to be Mexican.

It struck Ralph that if they wanted to catch McBride's foreman while he wasn't surrounded by a crowd of other people, then waiting 'til he was on the road to Santa Fe might be the smart dodge. There were eleven of them in their Vindicators gang and that should be enough to overpower the man; even were he to be in company with one or two others. There was no time to lose, though, because there was no telling how soon he would finish in the saloon and set off down the road.

The ten youngsters had armed themselves fairly comprehensively over the course of the morning. Some, like Tim Johnson, already owned pistols of their own, but others had never carried anything more lethal than a Bowie knife. It was terrifying to see these raw young men, marching round proudly with pistols tucked in their belts and rifles under their arms. Ben alone was not making an ostentatious display of his weapon. It was enough for him that he knew how to use the scattergun and had it near at hand. He was not at all sure that when it came to the point, he would actually be able to shoot a man with it; that was another question altogether. He was good enough at squirrels and ducks, but killing a human person was something else again.

Looking at some of the other Vindicators, Tim Johnson for example, Ben was quite sure that they would not hesitate to point a gun at somebody and pull the trigger. If they caught up with Angus McBride or his foreman, then it wouldn't much matter how squeamish Ben himself was about shedding blood: at least one out of the other ten would open fire. It was while he was watching the others showing off and acting the part of gunslingers that Ralph Moore arrived back from Mason.

98

As he rode up, Ralphie cried, 'You fellows best saddle up. One of those bastards is like to be alone on the road out of Mason in next to no time.'

'McBride?' asked Tim Johnson.

'No,' came the answer, 'him as calls himself Francis Xavier.'

'What are you boys waiting for?' shouted Johnson. 'Come on, Ben, you can ride alongside me.'

There was a mad flurry of activity as ten young men raced around like headless chickens, trying to get themselves saddled up and ready to ride. Ralph Moore was the only one of them who lacked a gun, so one of the boys who had greedily equipped himself with both a pistol and the matching scatter-gun to the one that Ben had chosen handed the weapon to Ralph.

'How in the hell am I goin' to tote this with me on horseback?' inquired the youngster plaintively. 'Won't one o' you fellows let me have a pistol instead?' But it appeared that none of them would.

'Here, Ralphie,' said Ben, 'I'll fix up a sling for you. Lordy, though, this here weapon's about as long as you're tall!'

When the troop of eleven riders set out for the Santa Fe road, they looked a rag-tag bunch to Ben's eyes. There seemed to him to be something rather comical about the collection of young men armed with a heterogeneous mix of weapons: rifles, shot-guns, six-shooters, knives and even one or two swords. That might have been how Ben saw them, perhaps because he knew these men personally and could not altogether take them seriously as real deputies. To an objective observer, though, one who knew nothing of the men, there was nothing in the slightest degree ridiculous about their appearance. They looked like a set of brigands or outlaws, and it would have been a rash man who went up against them. It was the very fact that they were young and untried that made them so dangerous. Here were eleven young men who would take any risks and stop at nothing in their efforts to capture the men who had deprived them of the next best thing to a father that most of them had ever known.

They rode out to the road which led north to Santa Fe. There was a slender chance that they had already missed Francis Xavier, and that he had left The Silver Dollar soon after Ralph had seen him drinking there.

'It won't do for us all to be in sight if that foreman comes heading up this way,' said Ben, 'he'll know for sure something's amiss.'

Eager to support his new friend, Tim Johnson said, 'He's right. Why don't all the rest o' you, 'part from me and Ben, go along over those rocks there? He's not likely to be afeared at the sight of just the two of us.'

Before they left, Ben said, 'Here, Horse, let me give you the warrant for that Francis Xavier man. You been deputized, too. If we stop him, you ride out and be sure to hold it up so he can see it.'

When the others had tucked themselves out of sight, Johnson said, 'What d'you think, Ben? Think we missed him?'

'I wouldn't have thought so. I've a notion that's a man as likes the inside of a saloon better than the outside. Question is, are we sure he'll ride his horse? No chance that he'll take the stage?'

'Not he! I heard him say as coaches are for sissies. Real men ride a horse or walk.'

The two of them waited there on the road, chatting in a desultory fashion about this and that. They could see some way down towards town, and would be able to spot any traveller coming from that direction about a mile before he reached them. Ben was more frightened and tense than he had ever been before in the whole course of his life. He sneaked a sidelong look at Tim Johnson, who sat in the saddle as relaxed as could be; like he didn't have a care in the world. Although he liked Johnson well enough, Ben couldn't help but wonder if this evident lack of fear was a consequence of the other boy's phlegmatic and unimaginative nature, rather than being a sign of great bravery. Maybe Tim just lacked the sense to know that in a few minutes, he too might be lying dead like Chuck Taylor or Pat Sweeney.

'Whist,' said Johnson, 'there's two riders coming along now. See, they just passed the stand o' trees there.'

'Yes, I see 'em. Can you tell if either of them are Francis Xavier?'

'Not yet. Look to me like *vaqueros*, though. What do you say?'

'You're a better judge of such matters than me,'

said Ben. He unslung the scattergun from his back. Cocking both hammers, he said, 'Well, it can't do any harm to make ourselves ready.'

His heart was hammering so hard that he wondered idly if it might burst out of his chest entirely. Was his fear obvious to the other man? Ben hoped not.

The truth was, Ben Drake had no interest at all in the man coming down that road, even if he did turn out to be McBride's foreman.

He knew, though, that if he were to achieve his aim of killing the man responsible for his own father's death, then he would need those other ten men at his side. If that meant winning their trust and affection by joining them in tackling the ones who had killed Chuck Taylor, then so be it. But Angus McBride was his alone.

'It's him all right,' said Johnson. 'We best not look like we're about to waylay him. What say you tuck that gun o' yours down a little out of sight?' he called softly to the nine riders hidden from sight of the approaching men. 'When I start talking to that whore's son, you men just trot out and join us, yeah?'

Then there was no time to think about anything else, because Angus McBride's foreman and his companion were almost upon them. Neither of the riders coming their way looked at all alarmed or even curious about the two young men loitering in the road ahead of them. Indeed, they were so bound up in an animated conversation which they were having that they hardly noticed Ben and Tim. Certainly, they had no apprehension of danger. Leastways, they didn't show any signs of nervousness until Ben Drake raised his scattergun into view and drew down upon the foreman. He said, 'Francis Xavier?'

'What is this, boy?' said the Mexican, more amused than anxious. 'Mind where you point that thing, there'll be some accident directly.'

Johnson drew his pistol and pointed it in the general direction of the foreman and his friend. At the same moment, nine riders emerged from behind a heap of boulders at the side and walked their horses slowly towards the little group in the middle of the roadway. Now, for the first time, the strangely named *vaquero* began to look uneasy. He recognized some of these men as ones who had been working for Chuck Taylor.

'What's the game?' he said. 'What do you boys want?'

As agreed, Horse, the only one of the party apart from Ben and Tim who was sporting a badge, produced the warrant naming Francis Xavier as a suspect in the murder of Chuck Taylor.

'What it is,' he said in a deadly tone, 'is that you, you bastard, are charged with murdering one of the best men who ever walked the earth. This here's a warrant, naming you for the crime of killing Chuck Taylor.'

'You boys are lawmen?' asked Francis Xavier and then he burst into a peal of laughter. 'Come, clear the way or you'll all be whipped and sent to bed without your supper.' He set his horse walking towards the men blocking his path. The man riding next to him did the same.

This was so unexpected that none of the youngsters quite knew how to respond. Actually, that was not quite true. Ten of them were at a loss, all except Tim Johnson, who already had his pistol in his hand and without any more ado, shot dead the man who had come down the road alongside the foreman. Faced now with eleven men who were apparently willing and able to use deadly force against him, Francis Xavier knew that he was outgunned. He didn't waste any time on words, but whirled his horse round, kicking up a cloud of dust, and then dug his heels savagely into the beast's flanks. His horse shot forwards as though she had been fired from a slingshot, fairly flying down the road, away from the posse.

As though in a dream, Ben raised the shotgun to his shoulder and fired first one barrel, and then the other at the fleeing man. McBride's foreman had only managed to ride thirty feet or so and at that range, the sawn-off was spectacularly effective. The spread of the shot with the shortened barrel meant that Ben was pretty sure of striking at least some part of the rider and horse with both shots. One took the man in the shoulder and side, ripping open the muscles of his right arm. The second shot took the horse full in the flank, gouging a hole a foot wide and bringing it to the ground, trapping the wounded rider beneath it.

The horse was whinnying and trying unsuccessfully

to get to its feet. The muscles in one of its rear legs had been shredded and it could not rise.

'It'd be a kindness to put that creature out of its misery,' said Ben.

'Which of 'em you talkin' 'bout?' asked Tim Johnson.

Angus McBride's foreman was alive, but badly hurt. In addition to the wound which he had sustained from Ben's scattergun, his leg had been shattered when his horse went down and landed on him. He was moaning in agony.

'You don't look so tough, you cow's son,' said Ralphie Moore. 'Don't sound too brave, neither. Squealing like a little girl.'

'Help me,' said Francis Xavier, 'for God's sake, help me.'

One look at the cold, hard faces which stared down at him told him that his pleas were likely to be in vain. He watched fearfully as the eleven men dismounted and then gathered round him in a circle.

'What sort of men are you?' groaned the foreman. 'Won't you do something?'

'Sure, we'll do something,' said Johnson, who still had the pistol in his hand. He raised it and fired once at the wounded man's arm. The ball struck the bloody mess where the scattergun had already ripped open the flesh. A spray of blood flew up from where the bullet struck home. 'That's for Mr Taylor,' he said.

One by one, almost as though it were some pre-arranged ritual, the other young men stepped forward a pace and discharged their firearms at the man lying with his leg trapped beneath the horse. With each fresh shot, the animal reared and screamed in terror.

Last of all was Ralph Moore, who was holding the matching shotgun to the one that Ben was wielding. It was, as Ben had justly remarked, almost as long as the boy was tall. Ralph had never fired a scattergun before and to be sure of hitting the mark, he advanced until the muzzle was only a foot from the Mexican's body. The boom of this shot rolled across the landscape. Ben thought that the foreman had probably been killed by the first couple of shots after his and Tim Johnson's, but he said nothing. If these men wanted to disfigure a dead body, who was he to complain?

Johnson said, 'We best put that beast out of its pain.' He paused, before adding, 'Meaning the horse.' There was a ripple of laughter. Nobody moved so Tim Johnson himself went up to the injured horse, spoke soothingly to it and then raised his pistol and put a ball through its head.

CHAPTER 8

It is a matter of common observation that the young are, in general, a good deal more cruel than those of mature years. This trait is even more noticeable when youngsters are acting as a pack. Taken individually, none of the young men who massacred Angus McBride's foreman were particularly vicious or unpleasant boys. When a dozen or so immature and restless men are working in concert, though, they are capable of terrible things.

After Tim Johnson had shot the horse, Ben looked at his hands to see if he was trembling. He wasn't. Shooting a man was not, after all, that different from letting fly at a bird or deer. Watching those others fire at the wounded man had been grim, but not unbearably so. When all was said and done, thought Ben to himself dispassionately, the man had almost certainly deserved his fate.

Having discovered that he was capable of shooting at and attempting to kill a man himself, Ben's main thought now was how he would be able to find Angus

McBride and exact private vengeance upon him. He didn't want the death of that man to be a joint venture like this. It was important to him that McBride would know why he was dying and for whose death he was being called to account.

Something which none of the others had seemingly thought on was that although three of them were supposed to be deputized peace officers, there hadn't been any real intention to take their first victim into custody. True, he had tried to flee, but after Ben had winged him, it would have been possible to take him into town and hand him over to the sheriff. Then again, it was the case that Sheriff Palmer was in some sense at least in cahoots with McBride, so that might not have answered. Ben wondered if the others were struggling with ethical and legal considerations of this kind. He looked at their faces and came to the conclusion that they were all untroubled by such niceties. It was enough for them that they had settled accounts with one of the men who had killed their beloved Mr Taylor.

'What about that other you shot?' Ben asked Johnson. 'Was he one of them as well?'

'I seen him around with McBride,' volunteered Horse, 'he was one of that set all right. Like as not, he was mixed up in Mr Taylor's death as well.'

'Question is,' said Ben, 'what do we do now? We got warrants for McBride's sons as well. Anybody know where they're like to be? I don't reckon we ought to ride down on his ranch, we'll find ourselves outnumbered.'

108

'Might not be needful,' said Ralphie, his face breaking into a wide and youthful grin. 'I mind I saw Alexander McBride outside the smithy, when I was in town. Maybe he's still around.'

'What d'you say, boys?' asked Tim Johnson. 'You think we're ready to declare ourselves? Let folk know that we're the Vindicators and we're a-comin' for the McBrides?'

'We're lawmen, ain't we?' said Horse. 'Why the hell should we not ride in and take him?'

They were all of them, apart from Ben, flushed with the thrill of murder done, as they saw it, quite lawfully. It was plain that the ten young men all believed themselves to have a perfect right to go and inflict death upon whoever they thought worthy of it. Ben was a little taken aback at this development. He couldn't see it ending well, because Joe Palmer would be sure to object if he saw some kind of posse galloping into his town and threatening mayhem and murder on the streets of Mason. Then again, he thought, some sort of ruckus in town might flush out Angus McBride and put him where I could take a shot at him by myself. A lot of chaos and confusion could help me. He said, 'Hell yes, why not? We got the law on our side, as you might say.'

'Well, what're we waiting for?' said Johnson. 'Let's go, boys!'

Leaving the two corpses lying in the roadway, along with a dead horse, the eleven riders set off down the road towards Mason. Ben rode at the head of the little column with Tim Johnson, thinking only of how soon he could disengage himself from the others and go looking for Angus McBride on his own account.

Alexander McBride and his younger brother Finley were sitting in the sheriff's office, talking things over with him. This at least was how Joe Palmer liked to think of these occasional sessions: as 'talking things over'. The two younger McBrides had less need to disguise the nature of these chats and described them to each other as 'giving Palmer his instructions'.

'What're you doing about those boys up at Taylor's place?' inquired Alexander. 'You given 'em their marching orders yet?'

'I don't see as I have any authority to turn them off that land,' said the sheriff. 'They ain't doing any harm.'

'They're squatting,' said Finley McBride forcefully. 'Living on land that doesn't belong to them. Turn a blind eye to that and before you know it, there'll be a heap of drifters and saddle tramps arriving in the district and setting up tents, camps, shanty towns and I don't know what all else. No, they have to go. You got to take a strong line with that kind of thing, right from the start.'

'Gee, I don't know. . . .'

'What don't you know?' said Alexander, roughly. 'You don't know which side your bread's buttered on? Want us to spell it out to you? Get rid of them.'

There was an uncomfortable silence. Although he was under no illusions at all about his situation,

Sheriff Palmer did not take to having it spelled out with such brutal directness, and was on the verge of kicking against the traces. Sensing this, Finley McBride sought to smooth matters over a little, by saying, 'Alex, what the devil is wrong with you? There's no cause to speak to the sheriff so. It's downright rude. I'm sorry, Sheriff Palmer. Listening to my brother sometimes, you'd think he's had no raising at all!'

Hearing his title used in that way, twice in quick succession, had the effect of mollifying Palmer, who said, 'I'll look into it and see what ought to be done. Not that I'm promising anything, you understand.'

'That's all we ask, Sheriff,' said Finley McBride. 'Only that you investigate the business and see if those boys have a right to remain on Taylor's property. Lord forbid that me and my brother here should try and exert any undue influence upon an officer of the law.'

'Yeah, well,' said Palmer, 'so long as that's understood.'

The sight of eleven heavily armed men riding through Mason, three of whom wore tin stars, was an exceedingly curious one to the citizens of that town. This was especially so, because until a week ago, these same men had been no more than cowboys, working on a local ranch. You had no need to be skilled in the arts of prognostication to know that the arrival of this band of riders was likely to bring trouble. Mothers who saw them gathered their children to themselves and hurried them away towards

111

their homes. Men on the boardwalks stared uneasily as the group of riders trotted past, wondering what was in the wind.

The blacksmith was no more pleased at the sight of the self-styled Vindicators than anybody else. He said, 'Seen both the McBride brothers here this day, Alexander and Finley. Couldn't say where they got to now. You tried The Silver Dollar?'

He had no idea whether either of the men they were seeking was likely to be found in the saloon; he was just eager to get them away from his own property before the trouble began. Because Tom Carter, leaning there on the hammer in front of his forge, had not doubt at all that some species of mischief was about to descend upon the town. His only aim was to keep it from his own doorstep.

They hitched their horses outside the saloon and entered the place together. Because they didn't know if and when they were going to come across the men they were seeking, the boys thought it prudent to carry their rifles and scatterguns with them. They presented a fearsome aspect to the drinkers in The Silver Dollar, who began to sup up swiftly, with a view to leaving as soon as was humanly possible. None of them wished to appear before his fellows in the character of a coward, but the truth was, nobody wanted to spend any time in the place when these young bloods were so obviously on the rampage and looking for violence. They might some of them be sporting badges, but they had the look about them of men who were seeking death, rather than taking those they were after into lawful custody. Later, when the bodies of Francis Xavier and Valentin Canalizo were found, out on the Santa Fe road, the drinkers who had been in The Silver Dollar that day congratulated themselves on their perspicacity.

'Anybody seen any of the McBrides today?' asked Tim Johnson of the barkeep. 'We've a few words to say to 'em.'

'No, son,' replied the man, 'they ain't none of them been in here so far today. That's not to say that they won't be in later, of course.'

'Son?' said Johnson softly. 'Did I hear aright there? I ain't your son.' He pointed to the star on his shirt. 'I'm a deputy, legally appointed and seeking men on sworn warrants for murder. Is that how you'd address me? As "son"?'

It was clear to Ben Drake that Johnson was growing into his role pretty fast. He would not have believed a week ago that the young man would have been able to speak with such confidence and assurance.

'No offence meant, I'm sure,' said the barkeep. 'I didn't see your badge. Those men you asked after ain't been near nor by this place all day. Deputy.'

'That's better,' said Johnson. He turned to address the bar generally, saying loudly, 'Anybody seen the McBrides in town today? We know they were at the smithy a few hours since.'

There was a shaking of heads and mumbled denials of having seen any of the McBrides since the Devil was a boy. It wasn't too hard to work out that

113

the less one became embroiled in this affair, the healthier it was apt to be. For a short space, the young men looked baffled, until Ben suggested quietly to Tim Johnson, 'You know, we're acting legally and above board here. Why not go down to the sheriff's office and set out for him how matters stand? Strikes me as he's bound to help us if he can. He's a sheriff an' we're deputy constables.'

'Say,' said Johnson, 'that sounds a right good notion. What do the rest of you say on it?'

None of the others had any strong feelings about the proposal, either one way or the other. That being so, they were quite willing to take their lead from Ben and Tim Johnson. All eleven of them accordingly made their way out of the saloon; to the enormous relief of the other patrons.

In Sheriff Palmer's office, the McBride brothers had finished handing out their advice on what their father expected of the sheriff. It had been a long list and Joe Palmer was, frankly, getting a little ticked off with being treated as little more than a glorified errand boy for the McBrides. He gazed idly from the window and then sat up sharply, spilling his coffee. Some of the hot liquid splashed on Alexander McBride's hand, causing that individual to exclaim, 'Mind what you're about there, you clumsy bastard!'

'Never mind that,' said Palmer urgently, 'there's a dozen o' Chuck Taylor's boys marching down Main Street in this direction. From the look of 'em, some are toting rifles. You men had best get in the back and hide.'

'Hide?' said Finley McBride angrily. 'Have you taken leave of your sense? We ain't hiding from that rabble of snot-nosed kids. I'll send 'em packing, you'll see.' He and his brother stood up and strode to the door.

The men walking down the street to see Sheriff Palmer were not in any special hurry. They strolled along in the middle of the road, like they owned the town. Until a few days ago, they had been just young cowboys, nobody to take any note of, nothing important. Now, they conceived of themselves as being men on a mission, men moreover who were backed by the law. They felt invulnerable and it was a heady and intoxicating sensation.

Finley McBride opened the door to the street and stepped out into the warm sunshine. His brother followed him. When their eyes became accustomed to the glare, they saw that what Palmer had said was perfectly correct and a gaggle of Taylor's cowboys were heading up Main Street in their direction. Some of the boys were indeed, as the sheriff had said, carrying rifles. One boy was holding a fowling piece and one or two even had swords hanging from their belts. The McBrides walked off the boardwalk into the road and took up positions right in the middle, so that the oncoming group could not fail to see them. Both were carrying iron, but neither thought it at all likely that they would be called upon to fight. It was too absurd for words, to see these youngsters, little more than children, playing at being gunfighters!

'Well, boys, what will you have?' asked Alexander

McBride when the posse was some twenty-five yards away. 'You seeking trouble?'

'We're seekin' you and your brother. We got warrants as charge you with murdering our boss,' said one of the young men.

This was an unexpected development and the McBrides didn't know for a second how to deal with it. Then Alexander said, 'You think you can take us down?'

'Shut up, Alex, you damned fool,' hissed his brother, 'don't go provoking them.'

'Take you down?' said Tim Johnson. 'Take you down? You see these stars? Means we've been appointed deputies. So yeah, I reckon as we can take you down.'

It was the last thing on God's earth that he wanted to do, but Joe Palmer knew that he couldn't shirk his duty. He would have to leave his office and sort this mess out. He was standing in the doorway, hoping against hope that matters would resolve themselves in such a way as his intervention was not necessary. It was becoming increasingly obvious with every passing second that that was not to be the case. He had to act.

From the doorway of his office, Sheriff Palmer called out, 'What are you boys about? Why're you waving guns round in that way?'

Ben called back, 'We've a warrant for the arrest of these two men, Sheriff.'

'A warrant?' said Palmer in amazement. 'The hell you have. You goin' to let me have a look at it?'

116

'Sure. Come right over,' said Ben, pulling two folded pieces of paper from inside his jacket. 'They name Alexander and Finley McBride as suspects in the murder of Chuck Taylor.'

Joe Palmer's not overly efficient brain was racing like some steam engine with the regulator removed.

'What in tarnation is going on here?' he shouted. 'Any of you youngsters have authority to make an arrest? I'll take oath as that's not the case!'

The McBrides were fast losing patience. Standing in the middle of the road, having folk discuss them like they weren't even present was not at all how Alexander and Finley liked things to be conducted. They expected to be treated with a mite more respect and consideration than this.

Finley said, 'You boys clear the way now. We had enough of this foolishness. You'll find yourselves in trouble, you carry on down this path.'

This wasn't precisely a tactful line to take when facing eleven armed men, all of them young enough to be hot-headed and aggressive. It was especially unfortunate when taking into account that ten of those young men had personal reasons for harbouring the most bitter and abiding hatred for the McBride brothers.

Joe Palmer knew, when once Finley McBride had spoken so contemptuously to Taylor's boys, that there was to be no going back and that bloodshed was all but inevitable. He ducked back into his office and snatched up the Winchester that he kept leaning in a corner for just such an emergency. It was ready

117

loaded and all that was necessary was to cock it. Then he hurried outside, in time to hear Alexander McBride shout to the men blocking the road, 'You boys ain't going to shit, then get off the pot. You take my meaning?'

This was enough for Ralph Moore, who called back, 'Yeah, I take your meaning, you son of a bitch!'

He raised the scattergun to his shoulder and fired at the McBrides. The echo ricocheted back and forth from the surrounding buildings. Being unused to the kick of such a cumbersome and unwieldy weapon, the charge of buckshot went high, shattering a first-floor window of the store next to the sheriff's office. Say what you would of the McBrides, they were none of them afraid to fight. Both Alexander and Finley drew their pieces before the roar of the shotgun had died away. As they pulled their pistols, they ran for cover, behind a cart parked across the road. Tim Johnson fired at them as they ran, also missing completely.

'Ah, shit,' muttered Joe Palmer under his breath, this being the very thing he had feared and been so determined to avoid. He raised his rifle and pointed it towards the group of men in the road, shouting optimistically, 'Throw down your guns, now!' For answer, two of the boys fired at the sheriff, both balls missing him, but one breaking the window behind him. He dived down and then snapped off a shot without really aiming. It caught Ralph Moore in his belly and he cried out in his high, boyish voice, 'Oh God, I'm hit!'

'You bastard!' shouted Johnson and fired three times towards where Sheriff Palmer was lying prone on the boardwalk. The first two bullets smacked into the brickwork above him, but the third struck him in the right eye, killing him at once.

Meanwhile, the McBrides were leaning round the wagon, taking shots at the boys in the road who, not having much experience of such things and being unversed in the best way to conduct a gunfight, had not sought cover, but continued to stand in full view of the two men who were trying to kill them. After another of them fell, a fellow known as Beany McPherson, the remaining nine fanned out and started firing everything they had at the cart behind which the McBride brothers were sheltering.

The wood began splintering and cracking; it would have been madness for either of the McBrides to lean out now and try to fire. Then a ball passed right through the side of the wagon and took Finley in the upper arm. He gave an oath and moved back a bit. This brought him into the view of one of the boys who was armed with a rifle and he fired at once, blowing Finley McBride's kneecap off.

Throwing caution to the winds and perhaps realizing that he and his brother had misjudged things in the most horrible way imaginable, Alexander McBride came charging out of cover, firing as he came. It was his misfortune that in the heat of battle, he failed to recollect that he had already fired six shots and so as he lurched forwards, there came only the repeated metallic clicking of the hammer falling on spent cartridges. He took three bullets in his chest and fell to the dust.

Finley, although grievously injured, was still trying to get up and fight, until a ball struck his head, rendering him senseless.

The silence which gripped the street, following the gun battle, was positively uncanny. Not a sound could be heard; even the chirruping birds appeared to have fled the scene. Beany McPherson was stone dead and it looked as though Ralphie would not be long in following him. Other than that, only one fellow was wounded; a clean tear through the muscle of the shoulder. It was bleeding freely, but did not look likely to be mortal.

Ralph Moore lay in the road, saying over and over again, 'I don't want to die, I don't want to die!'

The ball had passed clean through him, entering his stomach a little below the ribs and leaving his body via the region of his kidneys. No great medical knowledge was needed to see that he was not long for this world. So it proved, because while the others were fetching the horses, from where they were tethered outside The Silver Dollar, Ralph Moore lapsed into unconsciousness and soon after, stopped breathing entirely.

CHAPTER 9

The aftermath of the fight was a sad business. Two of their friends were dead and they had killed the sheriff too. Nobody on the streets seemed disposed to interfere with the nine remaining members of the Vindicators and no attempt was made to prevent them from mounting their horses and riding out of town. Beany McPherson and Ralphie were slung over their horses and transported back to Taylor's ranch in that way.

Although they had now killed three of those involved in the death of their boss, there was no sort of celebrating or satisfaction. The loss of two companions and good friends overshadowed their recent triumph. Being gunmen and settling scores with bullets was not quite the thrilling adventure that they had thought it would be. It was exciting enough at the time, but the aftermath seemed to be dismal.

Not having known Ralph and Beany as long as the others, it wasn't to be expected that Ben would be as upset over their deaths as the other men. Nevertheless, he was somewhat taken aback at how little he cared about the fact that they had been shot and killed in front of his very eyes. Beany, he'd hardly spoken to while he had worked for Chuck Taylor. He'd liked Ralph well enough, but was not really grieved for the loss of him. This worried Ben a little; he hoped that he was not growing callous. All he had been able to think of, really, since that private talk with Mr Sweeney, was the simple truth that the man responsible for his father's death was near at hand and still walking the earth and breathing the air, while his own father was lying in his grave. That wasn't right.

There was a pleasant shock waiting for them when they got back to the ranch. Three of the fellows who had decided to leave had returned, saying that they had been feeling like curs for running out on their friends, and wanted to stay and help them deal with Angus McBride after all. This was heartening, because it brought up the numbers of the Vindicators to twelve.

Entering the big house and taking the money and weapons which they found there had caused them all to rethink the sleeping arrangements. After all, this wasn't a church, nor anything like it. Mr Taylor was, God rest him, dead and would have no more use for his house. They were engaged in avenging his death, and thought that it would not be unfitting if they were to abandon the cabins and move into the big house for the next few nights. After all, there was no reason for them to live like beggars or hobos. They fetched the gear that was stashed in the bunkhouses and moved it all into the house.

That night, they held a council of war. The bodies of Beany McPherson and Ralphie Moore had been laid gently in one of the bunkhouses and the plan was to bury them the next morning. The sheer magnitude of what they had done that day was beginning to sink in and none of them were eager to go looking for any action for at least a day or two. For one thing, Angus McBride would surely learn today about the death of his sons and most likely about the shooting of two of his *vaqueros* as well. He would surely be forewarned. He was a rogue, not a fool; he would know that they would be coming for him next.

It was perhaps inevitable that after cooking up and eating whatever they could find in the pantry, the twelve young men began investigating the racks of wine bottles which lined one wall. It surely didn't belong to anybody on earth now and if they didn't take it, then as sure as God made little apples, somebody else would.

Ben Drake had no desire to drink. He had never been inclined to acquire a taste for liquor, having seen what fools it made of men. He was happy enough to watch the others imbibe the stuff, though. The drinking session had something of the character of a wake, because everybody fell to talking about the men who had died that day, both friends and adversaries. It was universally agreed that it was a damned shame that Ralphie Moore had been killed. He had been almost as much of a favourite as Fen Wilder. About Francis Xavier and the two McBrides, there was satisfaction. They had all been there when Mr Taylor had been killed so all shared responsibility for his death.

It was when conversation turned to Sheriff Palmer that there was neither exultation nor grief. Nobody actually disliked Joe Palmer, but nor was he exactly popular. The general verdict was summed up by the man who said, 'Ah, he wasn't a bad fellow.' His death was regretted, but not to any great extent. It was felt that if he hadn't tried to involve himself in their confrontation with the McBride brothers, then it would have been better for him and he might still have been alive.

As the wine flowed and the talk became more and more animated, Ben thought that it might be wise to sound a note of caution. He was full determined still to find an opportunity to kill Angus McBride by himself, but that would only happen if he was still alive in a day or two. Unless he missed his guess, they would all be unlikely to live that long unless they took some elementary precautions. They were sprawling round the parlour, a vast room filled with heavy mahogany furniture. Ben stood up and rapped on the big dining table which stood in the centre of the room.

'Listen up,' he said, 'I'd like to say a few words.'

'You goin' to make a speech?' inquired the nearest fellow sarcastically.

The noise did not subside. The men in the room were in the early stages of intoxication, their faces flushed and speaking loudly and increasingly foolishly about anything that came into their heads. He rapped even harder with his knuckles, but still nobody took any notice. Attracting the attention of all of them looked to Ben to be a hopeless enterprise. He tried once more, this time picking up an empty wine bottle and banging it loudly on the table. This did the trick, for the hubbub subsided and all eyes were turned upon him.

Ben said, 'I want to say a word or two and it's important that you all listen.'

'Important, is it?' asked one of the men sneeringly.

Tim Johnson cut in right sharp and said, 'You all listen now to what he has to say. If he says it's important, then important is what it is. Go on, Ben.'

'It's only this. Today, we killed McBride's foreman and both his sons. Not to mention where we also killed one of his cowboys too. Now I'm thinking as that is going to make Angus McBride pretty vexed with us.'

There were tipsy cries of, 'You got that right!' and whoops and hollers indicative of satisfaction.

Ben continued patiently, 'What I'm saying is that he might come up here with a bunch of those *vaqueros* and try and murder us while we sleep.' This time, there were no audible signs of bravado from his listeners. Instead, there was utter silence. It struck Ben Drake that not one of those eleven men had even thought of such a possibility.

After a pause of fully thirty seconds, in which time the notion sank into their brains, Tim Johnson said, 'He's right, you know. McBride hears about his boys' death, he might well come lookin' for us and this very night too.' He turned to Ben and said, 'What d'you suggest, partner?'

'Well, to start with, that we don't all drink ourselves insensible this night. And posting sentries mightn't be a bad idea, either. I'll take first go, for the next two hours. I ain't got a watch, but that there big clock will tell you all when it's time to relieve me.'

Ben was finding it far easier than he would have supposed possible to order and direct the actions of others. He wondered if he had some sort of talent for this, or if it was just the case that anybody who spoke thoughtfully and with an air of authority got listened to with attention. This was a riddle that he would have to think about once he had the leisure. In the meanwhile, he went a way along the drive leading to the road into town and found himself a good spot, overlooking the road. He brought with him the scattergun, which he had reloaded as soon as they got back from their bloody expedition to Mason. It had been arranged that if the person on guard saw anything alarming, then he would fire a shot to signal the others to turn out and come to the defence.

Sitting there in the darkness, Ben Drake tried to put his thoughts into some kind of order. Strangely, the fact that he had that day had a hand in the deaths of five men did not weigh heavily on his conscience.

It had surely been a novel experience, facing armed men and knowing that it was a matter of killing or be killed, but by no means a disagreeable one. The only regret he had was that Ralph Moore had died. He'd liked Ralphie. As far as Sheriff Palmer was concerned, he'd never met the fellow and could not feel overly worried about the man's death; unfortunate though it might have been.

Now that he knew that he wouldn't shrink from pulling that trigger at the crucial moment, Ben was keen to have a few seconds alone with Angus McBride, so that he could demonstrate in the most practical way exactly how he felt about a man who would hang another like a dog, just for getting crosswise to him. Ben had not deceived the minister back home, when he had told him that he was not setting out on the vengeance road, but now he knew the truth, he was quite fixed in his purpose. His sole, immediate and direct aim was to kill Angus McBride before going home to his grandparents' house.

The lonely hours wore away, with the young man brooding about his father's death and wondering how different life might have been had Clarence Drake not been needlessly slain. His childhood and youth in the home of his grandparents had not been a happy one and he was consumed by an overwhelming sense of injustice, that he had been deprived of an ordinary family life, being raised by a ma and pa, like other boys. There would be a reckoning for this with the man who had robbed him of that life; of that there could be no doubt.

Posting sentries throughout the night had been well thought of and showed that young Ben Drake was becoming a man to reckon with; not just resolute in action, but also with a mind that could plan ahead and spot dangers that others might miss. Even so, it was a fruitless exercise, because the danger that faced the youngsters holed up in Chuck Taylor's ranch house would not come directly from McBride.

Angus McBride was grieving for his sons, but even his grief was directed to a practical end. He wasn't a man simply to wail and keen in an agony of sorrow and regret for the loss of his children. Even as he suffered, he was working out the most effective means of revenging himself upon those who had slain Finley and Alexander. Riding down at once upon the men who had shot down his two boys did not feature for more than a fraction of a second in McBride's plans. Young as they were, those cowboys had already succeeded in gunning down his foreman, both his sons and also the sheriff of Mason. Now they were in a defensible position: a stone-built house. It would be madness to mount a direct assault on such a target. Well, there was more than one way of skinning a cat.

Over the years, McBride had built up a formidable network of contacts, which stretched all the way to the territorial capital of Santa Fe. The Governor owed him heavily, as did the Attorney-General. Now, if ever, was the time to call in all the favours that he had done for those men over the years. The loans that he had never called in, the vacations he had provided for them, as well as a hundred and one other things. He might not be minded to mount an armed assault on Taylor's house himself, but there were those whose job it was to do such things; men who were paid to attack fortified redoubts. If this wasn't a time for the army to act, then he didn't know what was.

Forty miles from Mason was a garrison of the federal army. It had been established after the end of the war and somehow never withdrawn. Although he was no lawyer, Angus McBride knew of the passage of the Posse Comitatus Act the previous year, which restricted the involvement of the army in civil affairs, but if the Attorney-General were to declare that a state of insurrection existed in Mason County, then the army would be forced to act if the Governor issued an appeal for help.

The next day, some of the boys had headaches and raging thirsts. They weren't accustomed to such exotic liquor as old port wine and it had not agreed with them. The events of the previous day had a dreamlike quality and they were hardly able to believe that they really had killed the McBrides and the sheriff. A reaction was now setting in and they had the sensation of waiting fearfully for retribution to fall upon their heads. To occupy themselves and take their minds off this anxiety, the whole lot of them set to to dig graves for Beany and Ralph, and make arrangements for the holding of suitable funerals.

With all of them taking turns at digging, it didn't take all that long to prepare graves. There had been some little debate as to whether or not both men could lay comfortably, side by side, in one grave, but the general view was that this would look pretty cheap; as though they couldn't be bothered to do the thing properly.

None of them had much idea about how to conduct a funeral so they fetched a Bible from the house and read out one or two passages. Tim Johnson wanted Ben to read these, because he said Ben had an 'educated' voice. The truth was that neither Johnson nor the others were very good at reading. Ben spoke a couple of passages out loud, those pertaining to the resurrection and so on. Then Johnson spoke a few words before they laid the two dead men in their final resting places.

He said, 'I knew these boys and I can tell you all now, they were pure gold. I ain't one for a heap o' fancy words, that's not me at all. But I say this. We whupped those McBrides yesterday and Ralph and Beany were there 'longside us. They done it to straighten out the score after Mr Taylor died, and we any one of us could have gone the same way. So goodbye, Ralph and Beany. Wherever you be now, we ain't forgot you.'

After this, all twelve of them took turns with the spades and soon filled in the graves. After some little discussion, it was thought fitting just to fashion a couple of crosses, by lashing pieces of wood together and planting them at the head of the mounds of earth which marked the last mortal resting place of the bodies of Ralph Moore and Beany McPherson.

After these exertions, they went back to the big house and ransacked the kitchen for vittles. Nobody had any appetite for further fighting that day, so it was agreed that in the evening, they would lay plans, tending towards finishing what they had begun, by going after and killing Angus McBride himself.

Very early on the morning of the day that the self-styled Vindicators were digging graves and reading the Bible over their fallen comrades, Angus McBride sent two of his men into Mason to roust up the fellow in charge of the telegraph office and get him to send a number of urgent messages to the territorial capital. These were phrased in such a way as to suggest that an armed conflict was taking place in Mason County and that civil law had broken down entirely with the death of Sheriff Palmer. These were despatched to the Governor and Attorney-General and signed by McBride himself. He made no mention of the deaths of his own sons, but referred to various agreements and understandings which existed between the authorities in Santa Fe and those in Mason. Angus McBride was confident that the recipients of these telegrams would catch the allusion to the obligations which they owed to him personally and would act swiftly.

The messages which went humming along the wires from Mason to Santa Fe were addressed to the personal residences of both the Governor and his Attorney-General, and caused great alarm to both those worthies. The pair of them were heavily in debt to Angus McBride, who actually held the mortgage on the Governor's very home. It was definitely in their interests to act quickly on such an appeal for help. Despite the provisions of the Posse Comitatus Act, the federal army was still obliged to act if requested to do so by the civil power. In this case, with no civil authority operating in Mason County and armed marauders gunning down anybody who opposed them, only the army would be able to restore order.

It should be said that Colonel Clanton Fairbridge, the Governor, was not at all eager to send an appeal of this sort for the army to intervene, but he didn't see really where he was left with any choice. Accepting all those favours from McBride over the years had left him and his friends in a tricky position. If it all came to light, he and his Attorney-General would most likely end up in gaol for corruption and bribery. It wasn't to be thought of. No, asking the army to deal with the mess in Mason County was most decidedly the lesser of two evils. Colonel Fairbridge briefly considered ordering out the militia, but that might look as though he were not being strictly impartial. Although Angus McBride didn't spell this out explicitly in his telegrams, Fairbridge understood that he wanted some enemies of his killed. Far better if the federal army were to undertake such a task, rather than a militia which was under the Governor's personal control.

A subject of such delicacy as this could not be dealt with by wiring an army base. The War Between the States had only ended a little over a decade ago and

132

the federal forces would not be likely to launch an operation without a signed appeal from the Governor of the territory or state concerned. Colonel Fairbridge cursed his misfortune in having become so deeply embroiled with McBride and resolved to free himself from the man's coils after this little episode was completed, but for now he needed to draft a legal document and get his friend, the Attorney-General, to check it through. It would have to go to the army base by special messenger. Could it be done this very day? Fairbridge thought that with luck, he could have the thing drawn up and delivered to Fort Worth before nightfall.

Tim Johnson found Ben sitting alone, on a little hillock overlooking the big house.

'Mind if I join you?' he asked, a rare act of delicacy on his part.

'Go right ahead,' said Ben, 'I was only thinking about things. You ain't disturbing me.'

'You got any plans?' asked Johnson abruptly. 'Meaning, after this is all finished and McBride's paid off?'

'I haven't rightly thought that far ahead,' said Ben evasively. 'What about you?'

'Me? I guess I'll have to light out o' the district. For all we're deputies, I don't see as they'll let us get away with killing a sheriff.'

'I've been thinking about that. There's nothing to say it was us who shot Palmer. We were just serving warrants and trying to take the McBrides into custody. It was all legal and above board. Who's to say

133

who killed the sheriff? Maybe it was those men we were trying to take in.'

Johnson stared admiringly at Ben and shook his head, saying, 'You're something else again, you know that?'

'I'm nothing special. And to tell you the truth, I'll probably go home to my grandparents when this is over.'

'So what brought you out here anyways? Most of us, we got no real homes to go back to. You turned up here and Fen Wilder picked up with you. But I never heard you say what you came to Mason for. You're not another saddle tramp, that's plain.'

For a time, Ben said nothing to the young man seated at his side. Then he ventured, 'Tim, you've been a good friend to me. I wouldn't like to deceive you. I got reasons of my own for going after Angus McBride.'

'The hell you have!' exclaimed the other. 'You knew him afore you came to Mason?'

'Not a bit of it. If'n it's all right with you, I won't speak further on the subject. But I'm telling you now, nobody has greater cause to hate that man than me.'

'You play it close to your chest and no mistake,' said Johnson, not in the least put out, 'but you're with us until we finish the job?'

'I won't rest 'til I see Angus McBride dead, I can promise you that.'

After Johnson had left, Ben wondered if he was being a little crooked. After all, he was hoping to catch McBride by himself and therefore cheating the other Vindicators of the pleasure of killing him. Still, he thought, anybody who knew the facts of the matter would allow that I have a better right to deal with McBride than anybody else in the whole world.

CHAPTER 10

As Colonel Fairbridge had hoped, the special courier carrying his appeal to the commander of Fort Worth, the nearest army base to the town of Mason, arrived shortly before dusk that day. Major Thomas read the impressively phrased, legal-looking document through carefully and then sent for his adjutant. When this young man reached his office, Major Thomas handed him the paper which he had just received and asked, 'What do you make of this?'

The adjutant read through it thoroughly and then looked up, saying, 'Isn't this likely to set us on a collision course with the Posse Comitatus?'

'The very question which I asked myself,' said the major. He looked vaguely around the office, the walls of which were lined with various books, document cases and piles of papers. 'Listen, do you think we have a copy of the damned Act anywhere? I don't much fancy going out on a limb for the Governor. From all that I am able to apprehend, he is something of a villain. I won't be made his cat's paw.'

The adjutant rifled through a box of papers and finally found what he was looking for.

'Here you are, sir,' he said. 'Want me to read out the relevant part?'

'Yes, get on with it.'

'It says that, "It is not lawful to employ any part of the army of the United States as a Posse Comitatus, or otherwise, for the purpose of executing laws". It means that we can't act like police. As we did during the Reconstruction, you know.'

'We can still act to put down an uprising, though?'

'Oh yes, we've a duty to do so.'

Major Thomas drummed his fingers on the desktop and then said, 'Have fifty men ready to ride at noon tomorrow. We're going to Mason.'

All that day, the men who had called themselves the Vindicators lolled around the ranch, recovering from the excesses of the previous night. After some talk, they agreed that they would ride down on Angus McBride's ranch after dark the following day and then deal with him once and for all. It was generally accepted that it would not be wise to drink at all that night.

The next day dawned as bright and cheerful as you could wish. The sky was blue, birds were singing in the trees and the only clouds were little wisps of white which scudded along gaily in the breeze. It was a day to glory in. The boys rose at a reasonable hour and breakfasted well. They had almost eaten and drunk the ranch dry and it remained to be seen how they would manage to feed themselves after that day.

The day passed slowly, with all the members of the band cleaning and loading their weapons. It was rightly guessed that this would be the last of their actions. Once they had finished Angus McBride, they would consider that they had done all that was humanly possible for the man for whom they had had such great affection, and would be free to see to their own lives and futures.

After a light meal at midday, Major Thomas himself led a column of fifty troopers out of Fort Worth. He detested paperwork at the best of times and relished the opportunity to be back in the saddle, with at the very least a little skirmish at the end of an afternoon's pleasant ride. The weather was fine and nobody could accuse him of goofing off. It was a perfect set-up. Best of all, if anybody later complained that he had been wasting his time on a snipe hunt, he could show them the urgent request from Territorial Governor, Colonel Fairbridge!

Before he left, the major said to his adjutant, 'There's nothing in the request from Fairbridge that indicates any especial location. I shall be riding straight to Mason itself and then seeing how the land lies from there. We'll head south-west, and skirt the river as it runs by a spot marked on the map as Grover's Mill. Then it's straight south into the town.'

Coincidentally, another body of heavily armed men were also making their way to another destination via Grover's Mill and in retrospect, it was all but inevitable that their path should cross that of the troop of cavalry who were travelling in the opposite direction.

At about six in the evening, Ben Drake and Tim Johnson led the young men from Taylor's ranch north to where Angus McBride's spread began. They were in no particular hurry so they proceeded at a walk. The aim was to reach the McBride ranch before the light had altogether faded, and then scout out a good point where they could conceal themselves until nightfall, when they hoped to attack McBride's house and kill him. After Sweeney's death, the Vindicators had abandoned all pretence at being engaged in arresting or bringing to court anybody. Their aim was simple and direct. They would shoot McBride dead and then go off on their separate and individual ways.

'You think we'll do it?' asked Johnson of Ben as they neared Grover's Mill. 'Meaning, we'll be able to kill McBride?'

'Don't see why not. He ain't untouchable. Saw that when his sons went down. Not to mention that foreman of his. He's only flesh and blood.'

'Yeah, that's right. You still set on going home after we finish this? No chance that you and me could be partners? You know, ride along together for a spell?'

Ben was searching for the words which would let the other fellow down gently, when he saw in the distance a grey smudge which looked at first like the smoke from a fall bonfire. Then he realized that it was not smoke at all, but dust being kicked up by riders. Quite a few, judging by the amount.

He said to Johnson, 'What d'you make of that, over yonder ahead of us?'

'Looks like a bunch of men coming this way. You think they're McBride's boys?'

'I wouldn't know,' said Ben, 'but why don't we head over to the mill there and wait to see what's what?'

Grover's Mill was a sawmill, perched by the river. Its machinery was powered by a paddle-wheel which the river itself kept turning. Wood was brought to the mill from nearby lumber camps, cut into planks and posts and then transported all over Mason County.

The twelve men reined in by the mill, attracting curious looks from the workers hurrying about. They could see at a glance that these were no ordinary cowboys and that something unusual was in the wind.

As the column of riders drew closer, Johnson said, 'I swear they're soldiers. Nothing at all to do with McBride. We're gettin' jumpy.'

Ben said, 'All the same, let's wait here 'til they pass. There's no purpose in drawing attention to ourselves. I wouldn't like to have to explain to anybody right now what I'm up to.'

Tim Johnson laughed and punched him playfully on the arm. 'You are one sharp son of a bitch, Ben, you know that?'

The cavalry came closer, but instead of trotting along the road and passing them by, the officer in charge gave a command and the column of fifty or so men halted. The Vindicators eyed them uneasily, wondering why all the soldiers seemed to be looking in their direction. The officer at the head of the troop trotted across the fifty yards which separated the two bodies of riders and saluted, which was a great surprise. He said, 'Would you men mind telling me where you are going? You look to me as though you are ready for some kind of lively action.'

Since none of the others appeared willing to answer this direct inquiry, Ben took it upon himself to do so. He said, 'Me and these others are deputy constables. We're on our way to execute a warrant.'

The officer looked Ben up and down, but not in an unfriendly fashion, saying at last, 'You're powerful young to be a deputy anything. I don't believe you're above eighteen years of age at most.'

'That's as may be,' replied Ben, a little stiffly, 'but for all that, I have a warrant here in my jacket. Would you like to see it?'

'Yes, please. Bring it over, would you?'

Ben walked his mount over and handed the warrant to the man, who scrutinized it closely and said, 'This appears to be in order. All the same, I'm going to have to ask you men to throw down your arms and consider yourselves my prisoners. If everything is as you say, then it's only a misunderstanding and we'll soon correct it.'

Ben reached out for the warrant, but the officer shook his head. 'I'll keep a hold of this for now,' he said.

Ben turned his horse round and then rejoined the others.

'What shall we do?' said Johnson. 'Surrender to them?'

141

'Why don't we just tell them no and see what they do then?' suggested Ben.

What was later known as the Battle of Grover's Mill was sparked off needlessly, when Major Thompson took exception to the band of riders simply turning their backs on him and walking their horses off; in effect, ignoring him. He was not a man accustomed to being ignored and took what he regarded as a pretty measured and limited action, which consisted of taking his pistol from the holster at his belt and after shouting a command for the twelve men to come back, firing twice over their heads as a warning.

When you're dealing with a large group of twitchy and trigger-happy young men, who have recently killed a number of people, including a sheriff, firing in their general direction is not the best move to make. Major Thompson of course couldn't have been expected to know this, and the first intimation he had that he had made a deadly mistake was when two of the men whirled round and opened fire at him. Only one of the shots hit him, nicking the tip of his elbow and inflicting an excruciating pain. The second ball missed the major but flew past him and killed the horse of one of the cavalrymen.

Without waiting for the order, a couple of the troopers fired back at the band of men, causing the workers at the mill to dive for cover. As for the Vindicators, they rode hard until they were behind the building of the mill itself. Once out of sight of the soldiers, they soon found that they were caught between the river and the mill. There was no way out, without going back to where fifty troopers waited for them. At Tim Johnson's suggestion, they dismounted and entered the mill. The men in there, seeing what they took to be a band of desperados or outlaws coming, took to their heels.

The boys found themselves in a cavernous hall, where the cut timber was stored. When they looked from the windows, they saw that the cavalry had dismounted too and were taking up positions around the mill. For Ben, the only sensible course of action now looked to be apologizing to the army and giving up their weapons. He had been all in favour of bluffing them and trying to leave without debating overmuch with them, but that bluff had well and truly failed. They would be unlikely now, after shots had been fired, to leave without finding out a good deal more about the Vindicators and inquiring searchingly into what they had been up to lately.

Ben was on the point of telling Johnson his latest ideas, when, to his utter horror, he saw Tim Johnson poke his rifle from the open window and fire at the nearest soldier. A dozen men at once returned fire, their bullets shattering the glass of the window and splintering the surrounding woodwork.

'Have you taken leave of your senses?' he shouted at Johnson. 'Name of God, what ails you?'

But Tim Johnson did not look at all abashed. He laughed and said, 'Ah, Ben, you're too cautious sometimes!'

It was at this point that Ben Drake knew with a

sudden and appalling clarity that if he stayed there with those men, he was apt to be dead before another twenty-four hours had passed. Some of the others, taking their lead from Johnson, were now taking pot-shots from the windows.

The troopers outside were returning fire with vigour and there was only likely to one outcome to the battle. They were dealing with men trained in warfare and outnumbered four to one into the bargain.

None of the other young men appeared to Ben to have the situation figured in the way that he had. Did they really think that they would be able to escape after this or talk their way out of trouble? There could be no question of all twelve of them slipping away into the darkening evening, but one alone might be able to accomplish this. It seemed a scurvy trick to play on these comrades, with whom he had fought side by side, but really Ben was more concerned with making an end to Angus McBride than he was in demonstrating his loyalty to a bunch of men he'd never set eyes upon until a month earlier.

Bullets were flying through the windows of the mill and the young men who had named themselves the Vindicators were sending back as many as were arriving. Nobody noticed Ben Drake double over to avoid being taken by a stray ball and make his way to the rear wall of the mill; the side which faced out on to the river. He opened a door and found that it led out on to a tiny jetty. Moored at the end was a rowing boat. Ben looked back. Still, none of the boys engaged in the fierce firefight with the soldiers besieging the mill had noticed his absence. He stepped through the door and closed it behind him. At once, the crackle of rifle fire became a little muted.

The dinghy was secured only by a painter fastened with what Ben recognized as a clove hitch. One tug would free the rope. On the opposite bank, bushes and trees grew right down to the water's edge. It was a pity that he would have to leave the horse, but at least he had the sawn-off scattergun over his shoulder.

For a moment, Ben Drake hesitated, his conscience and innate sense of right and wrong troubling him. Then he shrugged. When all was said and done, he owed the men in the mill nothing at all. He had fought with them and helped them and now he was heading off to undertake the object which was so precious to them, as well as him. Really, everything was square.

He gave the painter a tug and freed the knot. Then he stepped into the little boat and rowed across the river, being careful to ensure that the mill behind him blocked any view of him from the soldiers who were firing at the men within. He didn't want them to suspect that men were escaping from the beleaguered building or they would be combing the countryside for him.

As darkness fell, the soldiers had still not dared to risk a frontal assault on Grover's Mill. The men inside had apparently plenty of powder and shot, and were in no mood to surrender. The firing died down after a while, with both parties only taking occasional shots at each other when they though' they saw a movement.

Inside, Tim Johnson had been making pretty much the same calculations as Ben had, two hours earlier. He had noticed by now that Ben Drake was nowhere to be seen and had also figured out the reason for that. He didn't mind at all, although he could have wished that his friend had confided in him and bade him farewell before leaving. Johnson knew, though, that Ben was not just running out on them, but was even more determined than they themselves to put an end to Angus McBride's life.

Once night came, Tim Johnson was thinking that it would be a great game to race Ben to McBride's place and see which of them would be the first to get to the old man and kill him. He was still young enough to regard this whole exploit as some sort of juvenile escapade. Instead of slipping out without warning, like Ben Drake, Johnson thought it right and proper to let the others know what he purposed. There had been no shooting for over half an hour and the soldiers outside were seemingly quite happy to wait as long as it took; even starving them out, if necessary.

Johnson said, 'I've a mind to leave here now. The river's at our back and we wouldn't be seen in the dark. Any of you fellows can swim as well?'

'You wouldn't run out on us, man?' asked Horse, a note of entreaty in his voice. 'I can't swim. Don't leave us here.'

There were grunts of agreement from around the room in which they were holed up and Tim Johnson knew that in the face of such an attitude, he could not leave. Then the final assault on Grover's Mill began.

Major Thompson had his arm in a sling. He strongly suspected that the ball which had caught him on the tip of his elbow had chipped the bone. Whatever the precise nature of the injury, it was exquisitely painful. This, not unnaturally, had the effect of making his temper shorter than usual. He was starting to regret his insistence on leading this expedition in person. Maybe, he thought to himself, he was getting a mite old for such carryings-on.

Once the light had altogether faded, Major Thompson was left with the choice of keeping those men bottled up all night and starving them out, or simply staging a frontal assault on a defended position. All considerations of sound military tactics were against this second course of action. In favour, though, was the fact that Major Thompson was infuriated with pain and also that under the cover of darkness, some of those rascals might slip away and escape. In the end, it was the wounded officer's personal discomfort which carried the day and he ordered his men to open up with one last, devastating barrage of fire and then to fix bayonets and charge.

In the mill, it was obvious that there was going to be an attack. The firing from without was continuous; it sounded like one long roll of deafeningly loud kettle drums. Then it halted and Johnson could see shadowy figures rising from where they had been crouching and moving towards the mill. He wasted no time on further words with the other men, but simply sprinted to the rear of the storeroom and opened the door which he calculated led to the riverside. In his precipitate and headlong rush, he very nearly toppled straight into the water. Johnson paused for the merest second and then dived into the river, striking out for the opposite shore. The current carried him past the mill and by the time he staggered ashore, he was within sight of the troops storming the mill. It was dark, but one sharp-eyed trooper saw a slight movement and realized that it was somebody who had swum the river and was now about to get away entirely. He raised his rifle and took careful aim.

The total cost of the Battle of Grover's Mill was revealed at dawn to amount to twelve dead and fourteen wounded. These figures consisted of seven of the defenders being killed, along with five soldiers. The three surviving members of the band were taken into military custody. One of them, a young man who would only give his name as Horse, was wearing a deputy's badge.

Tempted as Major Thompson was to destroy the warrant which he had taken from Ben Drake, he couldn't quite bring himself to suppress evidence so blatantly. He raged at the three youngsters who had thrown down their arms at the end and sued for mercy, but the major had a strong suspicion that in spite of his promise that they would all hang for murder and treason in the end, they would all be set free. So it proved.

The warrant was properly and legally issued and one of the three men captured by the army at Grover's Mill proved on investigation to be an authorized deputy constable. He and his two companions had been engaged in lawful business and the fault for the bloody encounter at Grover's Mill had been that of the man who fired the first shot. All of which confirmed Major Thompson in his view that politics was the very Devil and that whenever he got mixed up in it, he always came to regret it later. It also proved to him that he had been right to mistrust Colonel Fairbridge, the Territorial Governor. This was a man quite plainly playing some deep game of his own.

So it was that after holding Horse and the other two in the cells at Fort Worth for a week, Major Thompson was compelled to release them and allow them to go on their way. He consoled himself by speaking these parting words: 'I know you bastards have been up to some kind of villainy. Never mind about badges and warrants and I don't know what all else. I know and so do you that there was more to the case than meets the eye. You may be justified in law, but you're still a set of rascals and I'm only sorry that I can't hang you all. Get on out of here, now.'

CHAPTER 11

All in all, it might be thought that the man who had ultimately suffered most from the activities of those turbulent days in the early fall of 1879 was Angus McBride himself. He had, after all, lost both his sons to the violence. No matter that he had initiated the fighting which was later referred to as the Mason County War, the loss of a child, let alone two children, is a great blow, no matter what the circumstances which led to such a bereavement.

Two days after the gun battle at Grover's Mill, which was the culmination of the brief war, McBride was riding round the perimeter of his ranch. One of the old man's strengths was that none of those who worked for him ever knew when their boss would appear from nowhere, and demand to know what they had been doing with their time for the last two hours. Any man unable to furnish a satisfactory answer to such a question was liable to be dismissed on the spot. It surely kept his men on their toes and acted to discourage idleness and slacking.

Although he was sorely grieved at the massacre of his boys, Angus McBride was not the kind of man to use that as an excuse for falling down on the job himself. He had been at the funeral parlour that very morning, viewing the corpses of Alexander and Finley. He had made arrangements for the funeral and had been furious to discover that he could not hold the funeral on the day that he wished. It turned out that those wretches, Pat Sweeney and Chuck Taylor, were due to be buried together on that day and, even in death, the two men conspired to baffle him and frustrate his plans.

The funeral of McBride's sons had been fixed for the day after tomorrow. It was a melancholy event for a man to be obliged to fix up, it was true. But that's what life is like. It is full to the brim of disagreeable happenings and unpalatable tasks. So Angus McBride reflected as he trotted his horse around the perimeter of his little domain. The boundary line ran through a small wood, half of which was on McBride's land and the other half belonging to his near neighbour. He was just on the point of entering this miniature forest, when a figure stepped out from behind a tree. At first, McBride didn't take any notice of the person, but as he came closer, he knew that this young man was not unfamiliar to him.

'Ha,' he cried angrily, 'what are you doing on my land, you young limb of Satan? Be off now, before I set my men on you.'

It had, thought Ben Drake, been a smart move to lay low for a couple of days. After getting clear of the mill, he had walked along in the dark until he struck a ford; then crossed the river and set off back the way he and the others had come. It would not perhaps be a good idea to sleep in Taylor's house tonight, but there was no reason why he shouldn't go back to it and take any food and other articles that he needed. He wasn't in the habit of sleeping out of doors, but he was sure that he could manage it well enough for a night or two. Behind him, he could hear the angry snap of rifle fire. It sounded very much as though the battle had heated up after his departure.

There was nobody at the Taylor ranch by the time Ben reached it. He had walked the moon out of the sky and in the east was the first glimmering of false dawn. Working on the assumption that it would be hazardous to linger too long, he raided the kitchen and carried off enough food to last him for the coming day. He felt dog-tired now and his main aim was to find somewhere that he might sleep for a while. At the same time, he had no wish to move too far from the big house: he might need other supplies by and by.

The ideal spot to rest soon presented itself. A half mile from the house was a hay-rick. All he would need to do was burrow down into the thing, like a mouse building a nest. Nobody would see him unless they were actually searching high and low. It was a perfect arrangement and as soon as he settled into the soft hay, Ben found his eyes closing and sleep washing over him. He drifted off in a matter of minutes.

That first day, Ben did not move far from the house. He half-expected that somebody would be coming out here to investigate after the shootout at the mill, but there was nobody. He risked nipping back into the house twice, once for more food and then again for powder, shot and caps. The scattergun had been splashed with water during his crossing of the river, but he had let it dry in the sun and it was ready for use again. Ben's only intention now was to see McBride killed and then to return with no more ado to his grandparents' house. It had been an adventurous time, but he was minded to live a little more quietly for a while now.

After another night spent in the hay-rick, Ben was convinced that nobody was hunting for him; or for that matter, the others. Surely, people would have come sniffing around up here if there had been any desire to track down either him or any of the other Vindicators? No, it was safe now.

That afternoon, Ben Drake loaded up the scatter-gun and fitted caps over the nipples of the lock. He knew roughly the direction of Angus McBride's spread and after eating all that remained of the food he'd taken, Ben set off with the fowling piece slung over his shoulder. He didn't know quite how he was going to go about it, but it was his fixed aim to settle with the man who had killed his father. The only thing nagging at the back of his mind was whether or not he would be able to kill a man in cold blood. Shooting at somebody when you are part of a group of men all firing and being fired at is one thing.

Under such conditions, shooting is apt to come quite naturally. This, though, might be a horse of another colour.

As he came closer to what he thought was probably McBride's land, Ben found himself approaching a little wood. It was a pleasant change from the dusty landscape. He skirted around the trees and ahead of him saw a splash of vivid red, which he at first took to be flowers; a rose bush perhaps. Then, with a shock, he knew what it was he was looking at. They weren't flowers at all. Two men were lying, one on top of the other and both were drenched in blood. He speeded up his pace and began to run to see if he could be of any assistance. His first thought was that he had stumbled upon the scene of some dreadful accident.

When he was all but on top of the two men, for so they proved to be, the one on top of the other turned a ghostly-pale countenance towards Ben and tried painfully to smile. It was Tim Johnson and he managed to croak, 'Beat you to it, man. Got here before you.'

When he was much older, Ben Drake became something of a fan of the Italian opera and he thought in later life that this little vignette, that he had witnessed when he was little more than a boy, resembled the climax of some extravagant operatic production. Angus McBride was dead; cut to ribbons with the enormous Bowie knife which Tim Johnson still grasped in his hand. Before he had been killed though, he had succeeded in drawing his pistol and shooting Johnson in the belly. Tim Johnson had already been wounded by a shot fired at Grover's Mill, but he had been damned if he would die before dealing with Angus McBride. Ben could see at once that his friend had probably lost more blood than he could afford.

Squatting down beside Johnson, Ben said gently, 'Can I do aught for you?'

The other man shook his head slightly and said, in a thin, reedy voice, very different from his usual, robust way of speaking, 'No. I'm all shot to pieces. Don't think I've got long to go.'

'Anything I can fetch you?'

'You can set by me for a spell. I reckon you was taken aback to find me here. I got here before you, see.'

'Yes,' said Ben sadly, 'I can see that.'

Johnson looked anxious and tried to raise his head a little. He was lying face down on top of McBride and looked pretty comfortable; like he was using the corpse as a mattress or something.

He said, 'You ain't vexed with me, are you, Ben? I know you particularly wanted to kill this bastard. I just couldn't wait, though.'

'Hell, I ain't vexed with you, no how. So long as one of us took him down, that's what matters.'

Tim Johnson let his head rest back down again, as though the effort of talking had exhausted him. His eyes were closed. Then he opened them again and looked at Ben, saying slowly, 'You never said why it was specially important to you to kill McBride. You goin' to tell me now?'

'He killed my pa. Years ago, when I was little. I came to set things right. But it's all right, you did it for me.'

'Hey, we're partners, right?'

Those were the last words that Tim Johnson spoke. He closed his eyes again and this time he didn't open them. As Ben watched, his friend's breathing became laboured and stertorous. Then he snorted twice, as though he was about to cough and let out a long sigh. He never took another breath and Ben guessed that he had died. So it proved, when he tried unsuccessfully to find a pulse.

These two deaths marked the end of the so-called Mason County War; which cost the lives in total of twenty-one men. Not that Ben Drake had been inclined to keep a running tally of the deaths, as they occurred. It was enough for him that he had preserved his own life and seen the man who had been responsible for his father's death lying dead in the end.

It didn't seem right to leave Tim Johnson lying there on top of McBride, so Ben rolled him off and set him aside from the other man; lying him on his back and folding his hands over his breast as was decent and fitting. He would have liked to say a few words over Johnson, something in the nature of a eulogy, but he was keenly aware that somebody might come along by at any moment and he could easily find himself held accountable for both deaths.

There didn't seem a great deal of point in staying any longer in Mason County and there were many good reasons for not doing so. Chief among these was the uneasy feeling Ben had that there might be those as would want to see him hanged; either for his role in the gunfight which killed the sheriff of Mason or for some other matter, such as the battle at the mill. All things considered, the best move he could make was away from Mason County and back to his own home.

It was late afternoon and Ben toyed briefly with the idea of going back to the Taylor spread and collecting some food. But then again, he had a few dollars of his own, which he had had no occasion to spend since fetching up in Mason over a month ago. That would do for vittles on his journey. He needed to be heading north, so he kept the setting sun on his left-hand side and started walking. He thought that it might be wise not to march straight across McBride's land, and he made a long detour, judging as best he could that he was keeping to open country.

It took the young man four days to get back to his grandparents' house; by which time he was as footsore and weary as could be. The good side of the thing was that he had plenty of time to think and turn the recent adventures over in his mind and examine them from all angles.

One thing he was glad about in retrospect was that he hadn't ended up killing Angus McBride in cold blood. Such an action would have sat ill with his conscience. It was bad enough having shot McBride's foreman; how he would have lived with himself had he ended up shooting a man down and killing him,

157

all by his own self, he really did not know. Not but
that McBride didn't richly deserve to die, it was just
that now it was all over, Ben was glad that the old
devil had died at the hands of another.

The most important lesson that Ben learned was
that he did not care at all for that way of life. Like so
many young men from dull and respectable homes,
he'd always had a hankering for adventure and wild
action. His childhood had been spent studying hard
in school and now he was about to go away to college;
or that at least had been the plan before he upped
and left to come here to Mason. Before all this, the
idea of college was a dreary one and Ben had pined
for the outdoor life. Coming out here had been only
partly about looking into his father's death; he had
been motivated too by the same spirit of adventure
which grips so many boys as they make that perilous
transition to adulthood.

After walking that day until it was pitch dark, Ben
flopped down under a tree and fell asleep at once.
Being young, his sleep was undisturbed by phan-
tasms of the dead or anything of that sort. His
conscience as he laid himself down to sleep was
remarkably clear. He had not actually killed anybody
himself. For all he had shot was that Francis Xavier
fellow; it had been the others who had killed him. So
that was all right.

The following day, the young man succeeded in
cadging a lift on a farm wagon heading along the
Santa Fe road in the general direction of his home.
Ben had tossed the fowling piece away on awakening.

From all that he was able to collect, the possession of such a deadly weapon was likely to cause him more trouble than it was worth now. It would have been nice to retain it as a souvenir of his recent adventures, but the main thing now was to get home.

'Where you heading, son?' asked the farmer. 'You just on the tramp, or you got some special destination in mind?'

'I'm heading home.'

'Where d'ye live? Up Santa Fe way?'

'Yes, a little town near there,' said Ben.

'What you been a-doin' in these here parts? Aught special?'

'No, not really. Just killing a little time before going to college.'

'College, hey? Ain't had much eddycation myself. Can't say as I've ever felt the lack of it. Be kind of slow, won't it?'

'No,' said Ben, with great feeling, 'I don't think it will be at all slow. To tell you the truth, I'm looking forward to it immensely.'

'Well, I guess it takes all sorts. Woulda thought a young man like you would prefer something a little more lively.'

'No,' replied Ben, 'that's the last thing I'd be wanting.'